My Mum and
Other Horror Stories

'Go and write about it,' said Dad. 'Go on, you want to be a writer – it'll make a good sitcom one day. You'll feel a lot better when you've got it off your chest.'

'I want to write horror stories not sitcoms,' I said.

'The idea of your mum on that bike *is* a horror story.'

So Kate begins her hilarious account of life with her well-meaning but eccentric mum.

Meg Harper has a varied life, writing, teaching drama and home-educating her children. In her spare time she enjoys swimming, walking her dogs, reading and visiting tea shops.

Other titles in this series: *My Mum and the Gruesome Twosome* and *My Mum and the Hound from Hell*.

D0191519

For Alan – with love and thanks

My Mum
and
Other Horror
Stories

Meg Harper

LION
Children's Books

Text copyright © 1997, 2003 Meg Harper
This edition copyright © 2003 Lion Publishing

The author asserts the moral right to be
identified as the author of this work

Published by
Lion Publishing plc
Mayfield House, 256 Banbury Road,
Oxford OX2 7DH, England
www.lion-publishing.co.uk
ISBN 0 7459 4830 8

First edition 1997
This revised edition 2003
10 9 8 7 6 5 4 3 2 1 0

A catalogue record for this book is available
from the British Library

Typeset in 11/16 Garamond ITC Light BT
Printed and bound in Great Britain
by Cox and Wyman Ltd, Reading

Contents

1

My Mum and the Day Out

I am going to die. Definitely. Without a shadow of a doubt. If I have to live through one more day like today, then that will be it. Finito. Curtains. The End.

'Go and write about it,' said Dad, when he found me gnawing chunks off my finger ends in the bathroom. I glowered at him in my best push-off-and-leave-me-alone sort of way but he didn't take the hint.

'Go on,' he said and actually had the cheek to give me a shove. 'You want to be a writer – it'll make a good sitcom one day. You'll feel a lot better when you've got it off your chest.'

'I want to write horror stories not sitcoms,' I said and didn't move.

'Well, change the angle then,' he said. 'The idea of your mum on that bike she's brought home *is* a horror story.

And for heaven's sake move! I want to use the loo.'

So here I am. Getting it off my chest. Wishing I could type with more than two fingers. Dad's quite right really. It will make me feel better. And I ought to write it down – the whole lot – everything I have to suffer. I mean, no one will believe what I've had to put up with for the last thirteen (well, nearly) years! Just think, one day it might get published to rave reviews. 'How did she cope?' the papers will say. 'How did she live for so long with that crackbrained mother and manage to stay sane?' I'd just better make sure that Mum doesn't find the disk before I've made a million out of it, or I'll be the one with the cracked brain!

It all started at breakfast this morning. I should have known better. After nearly thirteen years I really should have had more sense. But I didn't, so there we go. Or there we went. To Oxford, that is. Because it's half-term and because Ben (my little brother – he hates being called little but he is – he takes after Mum) and I foolishly said yes. Yes, we would like to go to Oxford and visit the Pitt Rivers Museum and have lunch at McDonald's. Doesn't sound too foolish, does it? It's the sort of thing normal families do all the time, no problem. But with our mum? You've got to be joking! Our brains must have been about as mushy as our Weetabix.

I first smelt a rat when I found Mum covering the front seat of the car with a sheet of plastic and a towel.

'Oh no!' I said, in dismay. 'We're not taking Gran, are we?'

'Don't be mean, Kate,' said Mum briskly. 'We haven't taken her anywhere for ages. It'll be a lovely day out for her. She's always liked Oxford.'

I groaned, but I knew it was useless. I should have backed out then and warned Ben, but I was still kind of hoping that for once we'd have the normal sort of outing that all my friends have.

Well, we picked up Gran from her nursing home and she was thrilled to bits. All dressed up in a hat and white lace gloves. I just hoped she wasn't going to wee on the nice clean dress she was wearing – she has a bit of trouble with her bladder and it really upsets her. (Well, it would upset anyone.) Anyway, we got onto the motorway all right. That's always a bit worrying with Mum driving – she leaves it till the last minute to move out and you think you'll have to spend the rest of the journey driving down the hard shoulder. Ben always shuts his eyes, but Granny thinks it's very exciting and can't stop giving advice. 'This red lorry's slowing down for you, dear,' she'll say, when we're just being overtaken by a very fast Jaguar. It makes your hair stand on end. I'll say one thing for my mum. She never ever tells Gran to shut up. She just grips the steering-wheel tighter and keeps right on. 'Prepare for take off!' cries Ben.

And then we had the first disaster. It was me that spotted it. 'Mum,' I said, trying to sound calm, 'there's a red light flashing on the dashboard.'

'Oh sh…!' said Mum and then bit her lip. She very rarely

says anything worse than 'Bother!' so I knew it was serious.

'What does it mean?' I asked worriedly. 'Will we have to stop?'

'It means the car's overheating,' she said tersely, 'but I am not stopping on the hard shoulder with Gran.'

'So what are we going to do?'

'It's only nine miles to the next services,' she said briskly. 'Just pray.'

That's my mum's answer to everything. Just pray. The funny thing is, it usually seems to work. I must admit, I haven't got her faith and it seemed like an awful long way to me before we pulled off the motorway.

'It's probably the radiator,' said Ben, helpfully, as we studied the extremely hot engine.

'I'm not entirely stupid, thanks,' said Mum, a bit snappishly for her. (That's one of the irritating things about her – she's always *so* cheerful.) 'I'm just waiting for it to cool down.'

Sure enough, we were out of water. Mum frowned at the car accusingly. 'Wretched thing,' she said. 'It's not that long since I filled it up. It must be leaking. Good job I'm going to get a bike today. It's about time I sold this thing for scrap.'

'A bike?' exclaimed Ben, in sheer disbelief. 'You're going to buy a bike? Today?' I just stood there with my mouth open.

'Yes, why not?' said Mum testily. 'This thing's falling

apart. A bike will be much better for the environment – and keep me fit. I don't go very far. I can borrow your dad's car when I really need to.'

Ben and I looked at each other and shook our heads in disbelief. Someone else's mum on a bike, yes. Our mum – no. Definitely no. You see, you haven't met our mum. Before today, I couldn't have imagined Mum sitting on a bike, let alone riding one. How can I put this politely? Our mum is… well… chubby isn't quite the right word for her, though her face is a bit on the plump side. And fat isn't right, because that would suggest she was fat all over – and she isn't, though there's no part of her you would exactly call thin. The fact is – and I really will die if she ever finds out that I've written this – that she's what polite people call 'pear-shaped'. In other words, she's got a big bum. So big, in fact, that when Ben was little he invented a name for her: Big Bum Mum. That's what we call her. To each other, that is. Or BBM for short. So we weren't over-confident about her chances of balancing a bike. But Mum is always full of surprises.

Well, BBM filled up the radiator and we set off again. She'd decided to risk carrying on. 'We'll just have to hurry up a bit,' she said. 'I've got a few bits to buy for some of Gran's friends at the nursing home and, with the bike to get as well, we'll have a job to fit everything in.'

We groaned. We should have known. Stupid really. Ever since we took our first trusting steps, we have been 'hurrying up a bit' after BBM. We should have known that there could be nothing as simple as a day in Oxford at the Pitt Rivers Museum. We should have known that Mum never does one job when she thinks she can cram in fifteen others.

Parking a car in Oxford is about as easy as walking on a greasy tightrope in a hurricane, but it's one thing that BBM is good at. She knows all the places to try, and can squeeze her car into spaces which look a tight fit for a tricycle (never mind an ancient estate car). Sometimes I wonder why she doesn't just park on a double-yellow line and pray, but she never does. Today she managed to park only five minutes' walk away from the Pitt Rivers, which, with Gran, took a quarter of an hour.

The Pitt Rivers Museum is a very peculiar place. There're lots of museums these days with hands-on exhibits and videos and interactive computers. This isn't one of them. It's more like a jumble sale in a cave. There's one big dark room and it's absolutely cram-packed with the weirdest stuff imaginable. You'd have to see it to appreciate it, but everyone I know likes the shrunken heads best. All except Gran that is.

'Oh dear,' she said. 'I keep telling them that my glasses are wrong.'

'But they're shrunken heads, Gran,' said Ben patiently. 'It's not your glasses. They're meant to be like that.'

'No one is meant to be like that, dear,' said Gran, in a very queenly way. 'I shall look at something I can see better.'

Which, of course, is how we lost her. BBM was busy looking at something else and we were much too intrigued by the shrunken heads to notice which little alley-way Gran had chosen. It must have been a good three minutes later that Ben realized she'd gone.

'I'm sure she'll be all right,' said BBM, refusing, as usual, to panic (though she was looking a bit twitchy). 'I lost you in here once, Kate, when you'd just learned to walk. I could hear you, but you were too small for me to see over the exhibits.'

That was her way of looking at it, of course. As she's only four feet eleven inches tall, she wouldn't have been able to see me over the exhibits unless I'd been the tallest fourteen-month-old on record!

Well, we searched everywhere, of course. We alerted the security guards and Mum embarrassed us hideously by individually interrogating every unsuspecting tourist in sight. But no one had seen our Gran. It was as if she had been eaten by one of the dinosaurs.

'Oh dear,' BBM said, at last, as we stood around forlornly in the lobby. 'I suppose this time I'm going to have to contact the police.' At that moment, however, they saved us the bother. Ben, bored with all the hanging around, had gone outside to scuff around in the dirt, as ten-year-old boys seem to have to do. Suddenly he let out a piercing shriek.

'It's OK, Mum!' he yelled. 'The police have got her.'

Sure enough, after BBM had maimed a few Japanese tourists who were foolishly blocking the doorway, we fell out of the museum to find a burly policeman escorting Gran towards us.

'Is this lady in your care?' he asked sombrely. (Rather unnecessarily, I thought, as Mum had flung her arms round Gran in relief.)

'Yes, yes, I'm sorry,' said BBM distractedly. 'I hope she hasn't done anything too drastic.'

'No,' said the policeman, 'but we do just need to return a few items to the museum.'

We followed his pointed gaze and Mum hurriedly disentangled herself from Gran's grasp. I think we were all expecting to see her clutching some priceless lump of dinosaur bone. Instead, she appeared to be wearing half the contents of the museum shop. OK, I exaggerate, but honestly, she was festooned. She had African bangles jangling from her wrists and rope upon rope of beads round her neck – all with the price labels still on them. She even had some sort of crocheted cap sitting jauntily on her head. How she'd managed to get out of the place dressed up like that is anybody's guess. It looked as if she could have taken a whole woolly mammoth, never mind a rotten old dinosaur bone.

Poor Gran was rather upset by the whole affair and very inclined to be rude to the policeman.

'Now, come on, Gran,' said BBM gently. 'We'll just pop those things back where you found them and then we'll go and get a nice cup of tea and a sandwich.' Ben rolled his eyes at me. I knew what he was thinking. So much for lunch at McDonald's; Gran would never cope with that now.

Meaning to be helpful, I suppose, the policeman tried to remove one of the strings of beads. He should have left well alone. Gran was not amused and, quick as a flash, elbowed him sharply in his rather flabby stomach.

He doubled over. Gran's pretty wiry and she was really upset. By now, of course, a little crowd had gathered and someone was soon helping the policeman up. 'I saw that,' said some busybody or other. 'She assaulted that policeman. Resisting arrest.'

Mum was looking a bit worried. 'Now, please…' she said to the world in general, and talking quietly in Gran's ear, began to lead her back to the museum.

At that moment, I saw something which made me wish I was as dead and shrunken as one of the heads in the Pitt Rivers. Coming down the steps of the museum towards us was none other than Chas Peterson, the one and only remotely fanciable boy in my year, closely followed by his charming and immaculate mother. I clutched Ben's arm. 'I am going to die,' I moaned, nodding in the direction of Chas.

'Oh, rats!' said Ben, in that understanding way he has,

and that just about summed it up. Now I am not a complete drip when it comes to boys. Fortunately, and I never stop thanking my lucky stars for this, I take after my dad, not BBM, and I'm tall and slim and quite pretty on a good day. Nor am I cripplingly shy, covered in spots or over-worried about my bra-size. And Chas doesn't go out of his way to avoid me. But would you want to be seen with your batty, shoplifting grandma by anyone who went to your school? I don't think so!

Now BBM knows everyone in the whole wide world. Or that's how it feels. I'm surprised she hadn't met that policeman on a holiday long ago in Bognor Regis. Or that he didn't recognize her from an abseiling course or a charity parachute jump. She's forever involved in some newfangled project or other. And she is somewhat difficult to forget. I mean, apart from her figure, which is unique, she has this very short, spiky hairdo which changes colour about every three weeks, and these sticky-out ears which are simply loaded with ironmongery. ('Maybe she's hoping they'll drop off,' says Ben.) Anyway, what does Mrs Oh-so-charming Peterson do but come bustling up, all sympathetic smiles and efficiency, and ask if she can do anything to help. Hang me if I know how they know each other. I mean, Mum wears psychedelic leggings and huge T-shirts with slogans on them and spends her spare time campaigning about trendy political issues. Mrs Peterson always wears navy and a hairband and spends her spare time pruning the roses.

But at that precise moment, Gran solved all our problems at one fell swoop. There was an ominous little rattling sound on the gravel and we all looked down to see that there was a growing puddle around her feet. Poor Gran! How humiliating for her. Fortunately, she looked about as perturbed as the Queen on a walkabout. I'm not even sure she knew what had happened. Suddenly the policeman found that he was needed elsewhere and the crowd of onlookers miraculously evaporated. Mum adeptly offloaded all Granny's finery onto Mrs Peterson to return to the shop, while she hustled Gran off to the Ladies and I was left standing on the deserted steps of the museum with Ben and Chas Peterson.

Well, what could I say? Gran had been virtually arrested for nicking half the museum shop's stock and then capped it by thumping a policeman and peeing all over the road. There was a rather long silence.

'That your mum, then?' said Chas, at last, without looking at me.

'Who?' I said, almost brain-dead with embarrassment.

'The one in the T-shirt.'

'Oh – er – yes.' I kicked at the dirt in a fair imitation of Ben.

'She looks a good laugh.'

'Well – she is… sometimes.' I surprised myself. It suddenly occurred to me that Mrs Charming Peterson might be immaculate but didn't look like a good laugh at all – ever.

That was all we managed to say to one another. Chas quickly produced a pocket computer game and I found that I simply had to have another look at the shrunken heads. Better that than standing there for ten minutes like a stranded lemming.

After that, the day was reasonably uneventful. We skipped McDonald's, of course, and had to hang around the bike shop for hours, trying to pretend we weren't with either of the older members of our party. The bike shop manager kindly stowed Gran behind the counter in an old office chair and she snored the afternoon away peacefully enough. Meanwhile, BBM beamingly persuaded him to change the handlebars on her bike three times before she declared herself satisfied. You can't say she isn't assertive. She certainly puts people where she wants them. I wish I had the same effect on her.

You will never believe the next bit. Never. You will never believe that a so-called intelligent adult would go on a special trip to buy a bicycle without checking that it will fit in the car. But that's what Mum had done. We trailed back to where she had parked earlier, only to find that, sure enough, the wretched thing wouldn't fit in the boot.

'Hmm,' said BBM, in an I'm-not-going-to-give-up-on-this sort of way, as we stared at the back wheel hanging dejectedly out of the car. 'I'm sure if we pushed it just a bit further we could get it past the back seat and you two could just sit to one side.' Dutifully, we pushed and shoved, but it simply would not move.

'Perhaps if we took it out, we could try it round the other way,' said Ben helpfully.

'Good idea,' said BBM. 'One, two, three, PULL!'

But the bike wouldn't shift.

'I think it's jammed,' I said. The bike stand seemed to have buried itself in part of the back seat and, however hard I struggled, I simply couldn't get it out.

'Let me see…' said BBM determinedly, but it was no good. We couldn't fit the bike in the car and we couldn't get it out.

'Hmm,' said BBM, looking a little anxious. 'We'll have to think of something. They'll be expecting Gran back at the nursing home soon.'

'We could sort of tie the boot half-shut and drive very slowly,' said Ben tentatively.

I looked at him as if he was a halfwit. 'On the motorway?' I enquired witheringly.

'No, idiot. On the old road.'

'Ben's right,' said BBM reluctantly. 'We can't stand here for ever. There's bound to be something we can use in the boot somewhere.'

Too right. BBM's car ought to be reported as a health hazard. It's crammed full of used tissues, half-empty juice cartons, broken cassette boxes, assorted clothes, odd bits of toys – you name it, it's in there. 'I am not doing housework on a hunk of rusting metal,' she says.

'It's bad enough doing it in the house.'

Anyway, today the rubbish was a godsend. We found a couple of old ties and a scarf and managed to tie the boot half shut. It still looked extremely weird, as almost half the bike was still hanging out of the back. We set off at a stately twenty miles an hour, wincing over every bump and rattle, but at least we were finally on our way home. 'Never again,' I kept muttering to myself. 'Never again.'

But the day wasn't over yet. We were just hitting the open road beyond the outskirts of Oxford, when one of those posh Land Rovers overtook us. The driver was waving madly in our direction and BBM obediently pulled over when it stopped. Vainly I considered hiding on the floor behind the front seat because – you've guessed it – in that Land Rover were none other than Chas Peterson and his mother.

'Can I help?' asked Mrs Charming, smiling encouragingly through the window at us all.

'That would be really kind,' said BBM, and before I could stop her she was arranging for the Petersons to take Gran back to the nursing home so that she wouldn't be late for her dinner, while we pottered along at a snail's pace. Chas didn't even wave as they whizzed off, having moved the plastic and the towel and Gran over. I dread to think what she must have said to them. Knowing her, it will have been a catalogue of cute stories about me and Ben. I just hope to heaven she didn't pee all over their Land Rover.

And do you know what BBM's comment on all this was when we finally got home? She tuned into the radio while she was frying the bacon for tea and caught a traffic flash which said there was a five-mile tailback on the north-bound carriageway just north of Oxford. 'Well, thank the Lord for that,' she said. 'If it hadn't been for all that trouble with the bike we'd still be on the motorway! And can you imagine being stuck in a traffic jam with Gran?'

I ought to be used to it. After nearly thirteen years, I ought to know that that's just the sort of comment you're bound to get after a lousy day out with our mum. After all, when she isn't driving us mad with one of her projects or rescuing old ladies from the arms of the law, you'll never believe what she does! With her multi-coloured hairdo and her psychedelic leggings? She's a part-time vicar!

2

My Mum and the Christening

Dad says that if you're a part-time vicar, there's only one job that your partner should do – and he does it. He's a hairdresser. He says that if you've got to spend half your life in black-and-white fancy dress, then you should have someone around to do something decent with your hair. Not that what he does would be my choice. Personally, I don't go in for tiger stripes or really short at the back and long on top, but Mum seems to like it and I can see Dad's point. Not that that's all he can do. He's very good at the old perm and blue rinse – in fact, he claims that the only reason half the old biddies come to my mum's church is that they don't want to offend him – even if they do make rude remarks about his ponytail and his earring! Actually, to be fair, he runs a very successful salon and the kids at school are hideously jealous. Just as well really. Part-time vicars hardly earn anything – we don't even get one of those fantastic old vicarages to live in. I get so fed up when people ask what my parents do and I say, 'Mum's a vicar and Dad's a hairdresser', and they always say, 'Don't you mean the other way round?' It just proves how sexist people are, even in this day and age.

Anyway, but for my dad's hairdressing, today wouldn't have been the most embarrassing day of my life and I wouldn't have just been told to 'Grow up or get out!' Thanks, Dad! Honestly, parents! I was only having a bit of a moan. They spend all day behaving like complete idiots and then expect you to take it lying down! Well, I'm writing it down instead. It made me feel better after that awful day out with Gran the other week. Maybe I'll make a habit of it. Then when they wheel me off to the funny farm, they'll know the reason why!

It all started because BBM had a huge christening this morning. It was for some local bigwig's grandson and, honestly, you would have thought it was for the Prime Minister. So many seats had to be reserved for all the guests that there was hardly room for the usual congregation. BBM, full of a bad cold, was fed up with the whole thing. She isn't very keen on doing christenings for people who never bother to come to church at any other time and Dad (who seemed to be doing the hair of everyone except the actual baby) had had to work two hours later than usual the day before. Ben and I, however, were quite excited. Thanks to Dad doing all that spraying and moussing, we'd all been invited to the bun fight afterwards, which was going to be held at a posh country house with a huge garden.

Ben and I were up bright and early by our standards for a Sunday morning. To our surprise, BBM wasn't up at all and Dad was busy ironing the white, frilly surplice she wears for church services.

'Your mum's not very well,' Dad said, shaking the surplice out critically before starting on his shirt. 'I've told her to stay in bed till the last minute. Can you sort your own clothes out, d'you think? And end up looking decent?'

Sensing that we weren't really being offered the choice, we wolfed our Weetabix, loaded the dishwasher and went off to get ready.

Poor Mum! She really did look the worse for wear when she finally appeared.

'I'll probably give this poor baby pneumonia,' she said glumly, as she stirred her Lemsip.

'Rubbish!' said Dad bracingly, who was blow-drying Mum's hair while she played with her toast. 'Just breathe in the other direction.'

'That's all very well for you to say,' said Mum. 'I feel so wobbly, I'll probably drop the poor sprog in the font!'

'You dare,' said Dad unsympathetically. 'If you do, I'll lose nine regular shampoo-and-sets, six perms, three blow-dries and a body-wave.'

BBM groaned and made a bit more effort with the Lemsip. It was no good Dad doing the lovey-dovey bit and sending her back to bed. Spare vicars are few and far between and there wasn't one in our town who would be available at such short notice. She was just going to have to get on with it.

By the time we got to church, she was looking a little brighter and anyone who didn't know her probably wouldn't have noticed the difference. Anyway, nobody was looking at her; everyone was too mesmerized by the forest of posh hats which had sprung up at the front of the church. Gran was enchanted. Dad had wondered about not bringing her with Mum being so off-colour but we all insisted that he couldn't be so mean. Gran had really been looking forward to the service. After sitting next to her for five minutes though, I was regretting our kindness. It was very tempting to grab her hand and sit on it after, for the umpteenth time, she pointed at some unsuspecting guest's hat, announced loudly, 'I don't like that one,' and went on to explain precisely why!

Three verses into the first hymn, I froze. It was difficult to see between the hats, but five rows from the front, wedged between the sort of man whose back tells you he's probably a bank manager and a woman in navy blue, was someone I was pretty sure I recognized. I craned forward to get a better look – and knocked the pile of service books off the ledge in front of me – crash! Half a hundred heads turned to stare, and, blushing madly, I ducked down to grovel around on the floor – but not before I'd seen that it was him. Chas Peterson. Large as life and twice as hunky. Presumably he was a relative of the squalling baby (the poor blighter looked miserably uncomfortable in a scratchy lace gown and frilly bonnet). While I was scrabbling around on the floor, I told God that if he existed he'd better make sure BBM didn't make a complete idiot of herself – or else! I still hadn't recovered from being shown up in front of Chas in Oxford over a month ago!

Well, Mum didn't do too badly – at first. She wasn't exactly sparkling and she had to blow her nose about every two minutes, but it could have been worse. All went well until she got hold of the baby to do her stuff – you know, the bit where they drip a bit of water over its head and make the sign of the cross. If a baby is going to scream, that's when it does it. Not surprising really. I mean, how would you like to be dressed up in an ancient dress reeking of mothballs instead of your nice, cosy Babygro, made to sit on Great Aunt Phoebe's lap amid a crowd of sniffy-looking strangers, and then have this strange woman in a white nightie make your face all wet?

Anyway, all the bigwigs and their friends and relations trooped to the back of the church, where there's an ancient font (that's the thing they put the water in). Ben and all the other kids stood on the pews so that they could see what was going on, while I tried to keep a low profile.

BBM was getting through it all nicely, when suddenly Dad gripped my arm.

'She's going to sneeze!' he hissed. How he knew I don't know but he was right! The next moment there was what sounded like this thunderous explosion, but it was only Mum sneezing (there is a bit of an echo in our church). The effect was cataclysmic! There was a great gasp from the people standing close by and a horrified female voice saying loudly, 'Well, really!' Then there was a ghastly silence.

'What's happening?' demanded Ben, who, as I said, is on the short side, like BBM. 'She hasn't gone and sneezed all over the baby, has she?'

'Ben!' I said, horrified. 'We're in church!'

'Well, has she?' he asked, completely unabashed.

'No,' said Dad expressionlessly. 'Only all over the baby's grandma, by the looks of things.'

'Oh no!' I said. 'I am going to die.'

'Don't see what you've got to complain about,' muttered Dad. 'It's me that loses the perm and the blue rinse.'

The confusion round the font sorted itself out pretty quickly. At least half a dozen men promptly produced large white handkerchiefs, while the women all rummaged around in their handbags. Poor BBM, though, was scarlet to the roots of her very short hair. It's at times like this, I thought, that I'm glad I've got long hair to hide behind. I sneaked a look at Chas Peterson through my mane. If

27

I wasn't very much mistaken, he was trying very hard not to laugh – in fact, halfway through the next hymn, his shoulders were shaking so much that his dad (well, I assumed it was his dad) elbowed him in the ribs. Oh well, I thought, at least HE thought it was funny – but I don't rate my chances of him ever speaking to me again. With a gran and a mother like mine, any sane person would probably try to keep me at a safe distance. I mean, what other embarrassing habits might run in the family?

Well, Mum got through the rest of the service all right and then it was time for her to be polite to all the visitors while all the regulars drank coffee and caught up with the gossip. It's quite nice usually, as I get to chat to some of the kids I don't see at school. Today, however, who should be lying in wait for me when I went to grab my biscuit and beaker of orange, but Mrs Charming Peterson.

'Kate,' she trilled, in her high, sugary voice, 'your poor mother looks quite peaky today. Is she all right?'

'She says it's a cold, but I think it's the flu,' I grunted, all too aware of Chas lurking not very far away.

'Oh, my dear, how awful. Will she be coming to the reception, do you think?'

'I expect so,' I said. 'She always seems to carry on, whatever's wrong with her.'

'Oh, I'm sure,' said Mrs Peterson. 'She hasn't changed.'

Hasn't changed from what? I wondered. Surely Mrs Charming Peterson hadn't met Mum on an abseiling course?

At that moment, Dad appeared with Gran hanging onto his arm.

'Here, take this to your mum and ask her how long she's going to be, will you?' he said, grabbing a mug of coffee and thrusting it into my hands. 'She should be in the vestry. Tell her it's time we were getting your gran back home, if we're going to get to the bun fight in time.'

I didn't need telling twice. I was only too glad to disappear before Chas's mum started asking Gran how she was. Knowing Gran, all the excitement would have gone to her head and she might at this very minute be under the delusion that she was the President of the United States.

As I was approaching the vestry (that's a little room where the vicars keep their fancy clothes), I was surprised to hear a raised voice. Now, you'll think me a low-down skunky sort of creature for doing this, but at least I'm admitting it. Instead of walking on boldly and knocking politely as I should have done, I looked around furtively, saw that no one was about, and then put my ear to the door.

'... a mockery! It became nothing but a mockery!' were the first words I heard. 'If you weren't well enough to conduct the service in a seemly way, then you should have found someone else who was!'

'I'm very sorry,' said Mum.

'You may well be sorry. I'm sure we're all very sorry. I certainly am. My brand-new suit is ruined. Ruined.'

'Perhaps it will dry-clean,' said Mum. 'Please allow me to pay the bill.'

'You certainly will pay the bill. Or for a replacement, if dry-cleaning doesn't help. And I'd like a letter of apology please. And one for my daughter. The whole event is spoiled.'

'I really am very sorry,' said Mum again. 'I'll willingly do anything I can to help…'

'You had better. I shall be writing to the bishop! I always said it was a mistake to have the christening here, and I was right.'

By now, I was fuming. How dare the old bag go on at BBM like that? How dare she be so rude? Mum hadn't meant to sneeze over her lousy suit and it was totally untrue to say the whole event had been spoiled. The family knees-up hadn't even started yet! Why didn't Mum fight back? Why on earth didn't she say how ill she was feeling and that it was totally impossible to find a stand-in at such short notice?

At that moment, I thought I heard a footfall behind me and whirled round guiltily. Well, I deserved what I got. Sure enough, standing a few yards away, studying me curiously, was Chas Peterson.

'Erm… I'm waiting for my mum,' I said lamely.

'Oh,' he said. 'I'm looking for Grandma. You haven't seen her, have you? The one in the lilac suit.' He sucked in his cheeks hard. I could tell he was trying not to laugh.

I cringed. 'Not the one…' I couldn't finish the sentence.

He nodded, wordlessly.

I winced. 'I think she's in there,' I muttered, nodding over my shoulder at the vestry door.

Just then, two things happened at once. A rather flustered-looking Mrs Peterson appeared from around a corner.

'Oh, there you are, Chas,' she said, sounding relieved. 'I thought I'd lost you as well as Mother.'

At the same moment, the vestry door flew open and out stalked a very frosty-looking old lady in a lilac suit, closely followed by BBM.

Either Mrs Peterson is very short-sighted or she assumes that everyone else in the whole wide world is always as charming as she is, for seeing Mum and her mother together she promptly said, 'Oh, so you've met! How lovely!' She turned to Mum.

'Jo, this is my mother-in-law.' BBM paled a little more, if that was possible. 'And, Mother, this is Jo Lofthouse – you remember, the lady who was such a help to me when I had that bad time after Daddy died.'

The silence was deafening. I wanted to curl up and die. I was just glad Chas couldn't have heard what I had heard. Mrs Peterson Senior drew herself up mightily and pursed her lips. Mrs Charming looked rather perplexed.

It was left to Mum to smooth things over. She smiled gently. 'We've already met,' she said calmly. 'Your mother-in-law was just telling me what she thought of the service. Now, I'm sorry to be rude but I must just check on my mother-in-law. She does get lost rather easily, as you know.'

And, slipping her arm round my shoulders, she hurried me away.

'Why didn't you have a go at her?' I hissed furiously, forgetting that I wasn't supposed to have heard anything.

'You were listening?' BBM sounded a bit shocked.

I looked at the floor and went scarlet. 'Sorry,' I said.

She gave me a quick hug. 'Oh, I forgive you,' she said lightly. 'But don't do it again, all right?'

I nodded and then, unable to resist, said, 'But why didn't you? I mean, it was an accident! And you're ill. And she'd no right to be so rude!'

'So you think I should have set her right?' BBM blew her nose, loudly.

'Yes. Why not?'

'And you think that would have made her feel better?'

I was irritated. 'No, but that's not the point – it's you I care about.'

'And do you think I'd feel better if I was rude to her as well as ruining her suit – and her grandson's christening?'

'But you haven't ruined it!' I retorted indignantly. I wasn't going to give up. BBM has this sneaky way of putting things, so that you start off thinking you're absolutely right and end up thinking you're dead wrong. Well, I wasn't going to be wrong this time.

Mum shrugged. 'She thinks I have.'

I glowered at her.

She sighed. 'Look, I know you're upset for me. You're bound to be. I'm your mum. That's the easy bit. The hard bit is being upset for her.'

I pulled away. She was going all holy on me. Any minute now she'd start telling me about loving our enemies. I had this nasty feeling I was going to come out of this feeling like a mean old scum bag.

'So are you upset for her?' I demanded crossly, trying to call her bluff.

She grinned. 'What do you think, idiot? I'm not perfect yet, you know.'

We had reached the car. Dad and the others were already inside.

'You don't fancy going to this reception on your own with the kids, do you?' asked BBM limply, as she fastened her seat-belt.

'Wimp!' said Dad, but he squeezed her hand and nodded.

'I say,' she said as we pulled away. 'I don't suppose anyone has a tissue, have they?'

3

My Mum and the Fête

Well, Chas Peterson's cousin (the one who was christened) didn't catch pneumonia from Mum. No, he was fine – it was Gran who ended up in hospital, poor thing. It seems really unfair, especially after she'd had such a nice time. Poor Mum feels dreadful. It took her a while to get better herself, so Dad didn't tell her about Gran at first. Once she knew, of course, she was off down to the hospital double-quick. She came back all tired and saggy-looking.

'I did warn you,' said Dad. He doesn't specialize in sympathy, but he made her a coffee and got out the chocolate biscuits.

'I should have thought,' said Mum. 'I was too busy flapping about that wretched christening. With her weak chest, she was just about bound to pick up whatever I'd got. She still looks really poorly.'

'She's over the worst,' he said expressionlessly, and that was all we heard because at that moment he very pointedly sent us off to get on with our homework.

We couldn't fail to notice the change in Gran, though, when they finally let her return to the nursing home. Her skin looked thinner and more papery and she had lost a lot of weight. Worst of all, though, were her eyes. They had always (well, as long as I can remember) been a watery blue but now they seemed strange and milky, so that she looked as if she belonged to another world – and, of course, in her own mind, she did. Before her illness, she made reasonable sense most of the time; now, she rarely did. The parents kept muttering about bringing her to live with us, but the Summer Fête was only a couple of weeks away so they decided to see how she was once that was over.

The Summer Fête might sound deadly dull, but in fact it's big business and raises loads of money for charity as well as for Mum's church. It seems to have grown and grown over the years and now it's more like a carnival than a fête. Of course, if you're a part-time vicar you not only have to spend months organizing committees of neat and tidy ladies and hearty chaps – so that there's tea and cakes, football tournaments, sideshows, bouncy castles, tugs-of-war etc. etc. – you also have to spend the whole day making a complete idiot of yourself. Usually that means it's a normal day for BBM, but this year she wasn't in the mood. Even so, she'd signed up as team-leader for the 'It's a Knockout' and had agreed to spend half an hour in the stocks. (That's where they throw sopping wet sponges at you.) I should have guessed that nothing would be that simple. I should know by now. Trustingly, I agreed to help out at the fête, little guessing that by evening I'd be chained to the computer, once again, 'getting it off my chest'.

Well, come Bank Holiday Monday, BBM and Dad were up at the crack of dawn getting things moving. Of course, because it's a holiday, getting people to volunteer to set the whole thing up is about as easy as cracking a coconut with a banana. Naturally, Ben and I had to do our dutiful children bit and by 8 a.m. were lugging things round the playing field.

The playing field, I suppose, is what helps to make the fête work. It belongs to the primary school but, as it extends right up to the church graveyard, it's the obvious place for us to use. There's a large, flat playing area which we use for all the events and sideshows and then it slopes gradually away to the river, so there's plenty of space to park cars. We usually even manage to fit in a car-boot sale, as well as all the other stuff.

By lunchtime, Ben and I were pretty exhausted – but there was no let up. We'd agreed to be car park marshalls for the first two hours; that way we'd miss the boring opening speeches. By the time we were relieved, the fête was in full swing. We rushed over to the events tent just in time to see Dad do a sponsored head-shave for one of the teachers at my school. Then I moseyed off to find something to eat and Ben went to rummage through the car boots. He's a junkaholic. He's convinced that one day he'll find something of enormous value and will be able to go on Antiques Roadshow.

I was just about to sink my teeth into an enormous and well-deserved hotdog when who should appear but Mum, looking like an overweight cheer-leader in her 'It's a Knockout' strip.

'Kate,' she said, seizing me so hard by the shoulder that my teeth clashed in mid-bite. 'I'm so glad I've found you. We've got a bit of a crisis with the "It's a Knockout".'

I glared at her, but she wasn't put off.

'You know the Fenhams?'

I didn't nod, although I knew exactly who they were. Mrs Fenham is a gym coach and her husband keeps doing extremely well in the London marathon. They are pillars of the 'It's a Knockout' team. I had a nasty feeling I knew exactly what Mum was going to say next, and I was right.

'Well,' she continued, ignoring my expression, 'they were travelling back from her sister's to be here and the car broke down – so they're not going to be able to make it. We need a couple of people to stand in. You'd be fine and I'm sure I can find someone else somewhere…' She gave me an encouraging smile. I was not taken in.

'No way,' I said firmly. 'If you think I'm going to make a complete prat of myself in a stupid costume in front of all

these people, you've got another think coming. Ask Ben.'
I took another bite of my hotdog and made as if to go.
I had already caught a glimpse of Chas Peterson at the Aunt
Sally and that settled it. It would be bad enough looking
like a dork in front of the girls from school, without having
him watching too.

'Oh Kate,' said BBM, obviously seething but doing her
best to remain calm and encouraging. 'It's for charity. And
you could be reserve if you like – but we've got to have
someone, and you'd be so much better than Ben.'

'No, I wouldn't. I'm useless at anything like that and
I haven't been to any of the practices. It's not fair to ask me
when so many people I know will be watching.'

'Hmmph!' snorted Mum. 'You're far too concerned with
what other people think! You know perfectly well you're
not useless. All right, I will ask Ben. I'm sure he'll be much
more helpful. And I'm sure I won't have much difficulty
finding someone else to co-operate either.'

'Ben's at the car-boot,' I said and turned on my heel.

Well, I'm quite ashamed about all that now, but it *was*
annoying and I did think it was unfair of BBM even to ask.
She knows how I hate doing things in public and she must
have known I'd feel like a mean old skunk if I refused. So
either way, I was going to end up feeling rotten. I stomped
off to find something to do, feeling so steamed up and
cross that I ate the rest of my hotdog without noticing.
(I was even more annoyed when I realized what I'd done.)

I ground my teeth. I'd as good as booked myself in for a serious little chat with BBM about 'why you shouldn't be too concerned about your image'. She has a jolly little verse from the Bible that she's fond of quoting. It goes on about the beauty of your inner self. Well, that's all very well for BBM; she's never had much beauty of the outer self to be worried about. It does make me wonder how she hooked a decent-looking husband like Dad though.

Anyway, at that moment, I was roused from my thoughts by some sort of commotion lower down the field. People were streaming away from the sideshows and tents to see what was going on. I heard Mum's name being bandied about and began to run. What on earth was she up to now?

Well, it wasn't so much her as her car. She had parked it at the top of the hill behind the events tent, rather than taking it down to the car parking area; she was using it as a changing-room-cum-store for herself and some other committee members throughout the day. Now the changing-room-cum-store had slipped its hand-brake and was rolling at increasing speed downhill towards the river. Close, but not close enough behind it, ran BBM and at least forty other people. It bounced and juddered over the hummocky grass but there was nothing in its path that could possibly stop it, and BBM bounced and juddered after it. It was just a good job that the parking area was some way over to the left. At least it was only BBM's car which was in danger of being rearranged. Most of the crowd ground to a halt after a hundred metres or so and waited with bated breath, but I ran on. I mean, it was a bit like watching a member of your family falling off a cliff; I couldn't just stand there and do nothing.

But there was nothing that I could do. Near to the river the ground flattened out a bit and became more rough and tussocky, but the car had obviously decided it had had enough. It was ready to end it all. Oblivious to the shouts and pounding feet behind it, it paused briefly on the riverbank and then slid gracefully down into the water. I could sympathize. If I had to put up with BBM driving me all day, I think I'd choose a public place to commit suicide.

BBM paused, panting, on the bank and watched as her car slowly began to fill with water. Its pursuers stopped too and stood around in a 'what shall we do now?' sort of way. It was an awkward moment. If we'd been wearing hats we would probably have taken them off. It almost felt as if we should sing the National Anthem or something. I just kept thinking about all the junk swilling around in there. And the stuff that wasn't junk but nobody had bothered to remove. Knowing my luck, the minnows would now be practising their arithmetic with the help of my calculator.

'Oh well,' said BBM, to the world in general, as best she could between great gasps for air. 'I take this as a sign that it was a good decision to buy a bike.' Everyone laughed feebly and the spell was broken. People started muttering about tractors and ropes, but Mum just shrugged and started back up the hill. 'It's a Knockout' was about to begin.

'Your mum,' said a voice I recognized behind me, 'is incredible! My parents would go berserk if something like that happened to them.'

I spun round, but the voice wasn't addressing me. A couple of yards away, Chas Peterson was speaking to Ben.

'Oh, that sort of thing happens all the time in our house,' Ben laughed wryly. 'You should come round some time.'

Chas shook his head in sheer incredulity. Well, that's what I hoped. Unless he meant there was no way he'd ever cross our threshold!

Then, ignoring me completely, they both turned and set off the way they had come. And do you know what? The vital bit that I haven't told you yet? They were both wearing Mum's team's wretched 'It's a Knockout' strip! I could have wept.

Sometimes I wonder about this God that Mum (and Dad, for that matter) are so fond of. One thing's for sure. He certainly never seems to be on my side.

4

My Mum and the Dead Cat

Our cat died yesterday. Well, that's the polite way of putting it. Actually, it got fairly seriously flattened by a kamikaze car driver. I wasn't exactly heartbroken; it isn't grief that's driven me back to the keyboard after only three days. I mean, all that cat ever did was hog the best part of the sofa, cry to be let out, cry to be let in and leave its hairs all over my clothes. Little brother Ben, though, was devastated. When Fergus didn't come in for tea last night, he was all for ringing the police and spent a good hour riding round the neighbourhood on his bike looking for him. Mum and Dad virtually had to nail him to his bed for the night and then he cried himself to sleep. It's a good job he didn't find Fergus, though. A neighbour brought him in this morning, wrapped in an old towel with just his head sticking out, and strict instructions not to look inside. Poor

Ben. Even after half a packet of chocolate digestives, he was still crying.

'It's not fair,' he kept saying. 'Fergus wasn't an old cat. God shouldn't have let him die.'

'Don't be silly,' I said, exasperated and running out of sympathy. 'It's not God's fault if some stupid maniac of a driver comes tearing down the road just when Fergus decides to go out on the razzle.'

Ben stopped crying for a moment and glared at me. 'Fergus was a very home-loving cat. He didn't go out on the razzle. He wasn't that sort.'

'Huh,' I snorted. 'Only 'cos he didn't still have all his bits. If he had, you wouldn't have seen him for dust. He had the look.'

'No, he didn't,' retorted Ben furiously. 'He loved us. He was the nicest cat there ever was and…' (at this point his face lightened) 'we ought to have a funeral for him.'

Mum and I looked at each other and groaned. 'Oh, grow up, Ben,' I said. 'Cats don't have funerals.'

'Well, they should,' said Ben firmly. 'With the proper words and songs and flowers and everything.'

'I don't think the words in the book I use are very suitable for cats,' said Mum dubiously, but Ben's lip was beginning to tremble again and he had a mulish look in his eye. 'Look,' Mum said quickly, 'if you can sort out the grave and the coffin and the flowers and everything, I could try and find some suitable words this afternoon – but it can't be a great long service, OK? I've got a lot of work to do.'

Ben nodded. 'Kate will have to sing,' he said obstinately.

I looked at him in sheer disbelief. 'I am not,' I said firmly, 'singing at a cat's funeral. Anyway, why d'you need me? Can't just you and Mum sing?'

'I'm too upset,' said Ben, with decision, 'and you can't have only the vicar singing.'

I opened my mouth but caught Mum's eye and shut it again. Ben's a great brother on the whole, but when he gets a bee in his bonnet about something, it's simply not worth putting up a fight. Nine times out of ten, he forgets what he was so upset about by the time he's eaten his next meal, anyway.

'OK, I'll sing,' I agreed, 'as long as I don't have to do anything else. If you want someone to make Fergus a shroud, don't look at me!'

Then I went off to play tennis at the local courts with some kids from school and promptly forgot about poor old Fergus and his funeral.

I was reminded at lunch-time.

'Have you been practising?' Ben suddenly demanded across the kitchen table.

'Practising what? My serve?' I said idly, rocking back on my chair as I savoured my mouthful of bread and cheese. I was still glorying in a couple of fine aces I had brought off that morning. Watch out Wimbledon, here I come!

His answer rocketed me back to earth with a thud.

'Your singing, of course. For Fergus's funeral. We're having it at two o'clock.'

I gnashed my teeth. The wretch was determined then. 'Course he was hardly likely to forget – there was still a dead cat in the garage.

'You haven't told me what you want me to sing,' I said waspishly.

Ben stared. '"Abide with me", of course. They always have it at funerals on the telly. I thought it was obvious.'

I gave him the pitiful look; the one I reserve for the really seriously deranged. 'It's only obvious to a complete half-brain like you,' I said, just in case he wasn't sure how low an opinion I had of him. 'You cannot sing "Abide with me" at a cat's funeral. I cannot. I will not.'

'I don't see why not,' said Ben belligerently. 'It's all nice and slow and mournful. And I feel mournful, even if you don't. And I don't see how I can be a complete half-brain. If I've only got half a brain, how can it be complete? Huh?'

I ignored the last bit and glared at him witheringly.

'It's not the music that's the problem, pea-brain,' I said. 'It's the words. They're too deep and meaningful for a cat. You'd be better off singing "All things bright and beautiful". That goes on about nature and stuff.'

'You can't sing that at a funeral!' Ben protested. 'You sing that at Harvest Festivals. It's a happy song! And how d'you know cats aren't deep and meaningful? The Egyptians thought they were gods!'

'Well, go and build a pyramid for Fergus then,' I snarled, beginning to lose my temper. 'Let me know when it's ready – if you've finished before it's time for your own funeral, that is.'

At that moment, BBM appeared. She'd been upstairs making a few private phone calls.

'What's all the bickering about?' she asked. 'I could hear you from the landing.'

I pursed my lips and rocked backwards. Ben could tell her his crack-brained scheme himself.

He was only too willing, of course. 'She won't sing "Abide with me" at Fergus's funeral. She says it's too deep and meaningful for a cat. She thinks we should sing "All things bright and beautiful" – at a funeral! It would be sacrifice.'

'Do you mean sacrilege?' asked Mum gently.

'Probably. I don't know,' said Ben, all red in the face and flustered by now. I had a nasty suspicion he was about to start crying again.

BBM gave me a look. It was a 'you'd better keep quiet if you know what's good for you' sort of look. You don't mess with that sort of look. I kept quiet.

'Why don't we get the hymn-book out and see what it actually says?' she suggested sweetly. 'I can't really remember, offhand.'

Ben beamed at her and raced off promptly to rummage through the pile on top of the piano. BBM looked at me sideways.

'Couldn't you stretch a point, Kate?' she said meaningfully. 'I don't suppose God minds if the words don't strictly apply to cats. Love covers over a...'

'Multitude of sins,' I finished for her rudely. That's another of her favourite Bible verses. But I was blowed if I was going to give in now.

Ben reappeared and plonked the hymn-book down amid the crumbs. We scoured the words closely.

'Doesn't make much sense to me,' said Ben, shrugging his shoulders.

'Well, it does to me,' I said triumphantly, 'and the last verse is definitely about going to heaven – so it's no good for a cat!' I slammed the book shut.

'Why not?' said Ben blankly.

I sighed. 'People go to heaven,' I said slowly, in case he had any difficulty understanding. 'Animals don't.'

'Why not?' said Ben again.

Oh dear, he was being very dim! 'Because,' I said, almost spelling the words out by now, 'they don't have the sort of brains which understand about God. And if they can't believe in God, how can they go to heaven?'

'How do you know what sort of brains animals have, clever clogs?' demanded Ben. 'Changed your name to David Attenborough, have you?' He wasn't giving in that easily.

'Yes, how do you know?' BBM paused in the middle of spreading margarine on her bread and looked up.

I stared. Whose side was she on? I thought part-time vicars were supposed to know about these things. Perhaps dead cats don't get covered in their training.

'I just know,' I said lamely.

'Oh,' said BBM.

'Well, I don't get it,' said Ben. 'I thought heaven was supposed to be a happy place. How am I supposed to be happy if Fergus isn't there?'

I snorted. 'You'll have forgotten Fergus by the time you die,' I insisted.

'Not if I die tomorrow,' said Ben firmly. He looked positively smug. I don't suppose he really gave a fig whether Fergus went to heaven or not; he was just in the mood for an argument.

Well, I'd had enough. 'What do you think, then, Mum?' I asked, pretty humbly for me.

She chewed thoughtfully for a moment. 'I think,' she said carefully, 'I think that's not a question we can answer. Sorry.'

'Oh,' I said. I don't know – what does she think she gets paid for? What sort of an answer was that? I mean, really!

'So d'you think Fergus is all right?' Ben said in a small voice. All the fight had suddenly gone out of him. He was obviously back to thinking about the sad little bundle in the garage.

Mum pulled her chair close and wrapped her arm round him. 'What do you think, Ben? Don't you think if God cared enough to make a beautiful cat like Fergus, he cares enough to sort out what happens to him when he dies?'

Ben gave a sort of half-smile. 'Do you?' he asked, snuggling against her (Mum is very cuddly).

'I reckon God can handle it,' she said.

'So can we sing "Abide with me", then?'

She laughed. 'It's not up to the vicar to choose,' she said. And then, looking at me, 'And the choir always sings what it's told to.'

So that is how, at ten past two, on a glorious, hot, late August afternoon, Ben, BBM and I came to be standing round a small hole in our back garden, alongside which lay a cat-sized, cardboard coffin. It was very professional-looking, apart from the bit where Ben had tried to paint out the words Salon Mousse and hadn't quite succeeded. On top of the coffin was a small bouquet of wilting dandelions – no other flowers grow in our garden. 'We never have time to sit in it anyway,' says Mum.

Now that's a really irritating thing about BBM. The way she always manages to twist things. 'We never have time to sit in it' is just a good excuse for total neglect. It would be more honest to admit that any plant she touches, she kills – unless it happens to be stinging nettles, bindweed, ground elder or, of course, dandelions. All those notorious weeds thrive under her care. It drives the neighbours mad; there they are, manicuring their lawns and massaging their rose-bushes and there's our mum, cultivating clouds of dandelion fluff to blow over their hedges. I'm sure if it wasn't for her job she'd have been poisoned with her own deadly nightshade by old Mr Ponsonby next-door by now. It's surprising in one so environmentally friendly, of course. I mean, by rights she ought to have her own organic vegetable plot out the back, but although she's very good at recycling anything that stands still long enough, gardening is out of her league. She does feel a bit guilty about it – well, very guilty. A few months ago she bought one of those wormery things – you know, TURN YOUR KITCHEN WASTE INTO NUTRITIOUS COMPOST WITH THE HELP OF A FEW TIGER WORMS – or so the adverts claim.

'What do we need compost for?' asked Dad dubiously.

'We don't,' said Mum. (She'd thought of that one.) 'We can give it away to keen gardeners. It's shameful how much kitchen waste we just throw away.'

Well, there's no stopping Mum once she's got a project in mind. The wormery duly arrived and we dutifully filled it with our waste. All went well at first and the worms settled in happily to their cosy new home. 'Well done, love,' said Dad. 'Those worms are the first things you've managed to keep alive since I married you.' She glowered at him. 'Apart from the kids, that is,' he added hastily before she was tempted to kick him.

Then the hot weather started.

'Mum,' said Ben, one day as he came in after feeding the worms. 'They don't seem to be doing much at the moment. The waste level isn't going down at all.'

'Oh, they're probably a bit sleepy with the heat,' said BBM. 'I shouldn't worry.'

Ben didn't look convinced but, as he said later, he didn't fancy poking through a pile of festering potato peel and left-over baked beans in search of critically ill tiger worms.

'Mum,' he said, a few days later. 'Are you sure it didn't say anything in the instructions about keeping the Wormery in a cool place?'

'Don't think so,' said BBM. (She never reads instructions unless they're from God.) 'Why?'

For reply, he held up what appeared to be a fossilized bootlace.

'Oh,' said BBM, as she peered at it anxiously. 'Are there any more like that?'

'Don't know,' said Ben. 'You look.'

Well, you can guess what had happened. The poor old worms had been roasted to death. 'Sensitive to extremes of temperature' the instructions said. There ought to be a law against people like BBM. Honestly. Now she's talking about getting a Vietnamese pot-bellied pig to eat up the kitchen waste. I suppose she'll be wanting to give pig muck to the neighbours for their roses. 'I'm not interested in sun-cured bacon,' said Dad witheringly, the last time she suggested it – but she sneaked home a book on pig rearing from the library last time we went, so I suspect we haven't heard the last of it.

Anyway, that's why we were standing amid the stinging nettles with only a few dandelions for a floral tribute to Fergus. Come to think of it, we were jolly lucky Ben didn't insist on a funeral for the worms. I wonder if they go to heaven?

BBM looked a bit sun-cured herself, actually. On top of her ordinary clothes, she was wearing her huge black cloak with the silver clasp and chain at the neck. It looks like something out of a horror movie and she normally only wears it for funerals in the middle of winter. She says it's the only bit of a vicar's get-up she actually wanted. Ben wants it too. He's been trying to get his thieving hands on it since his Batman craze when he was three years old, but so far BBM has been distinctly mean about it.

When she appeared at the graveside just after two o'clock, she wasn't actually wearing it. In fact, she wasn't wearing anything remotely vicarish or funereal at all. She had on a pair of shorts which looked like they'd been made from left-over deck-chair canvas and one of those T-shirts from Fat Willy's Surf Shack. (Question: Who is Fat Willy and what's so special about his Surf Shack?)

'You do not,' said Ben pointedly, 'look like you're going to a funeral.'

BBM had the grace to look humbled. 'Well, the T-shirt's black,' she said apologetically.

'With psychedelic writing on it!' said Ben crushingly. 'You should be wearing your black cape.'

'On a day like this?' protested BBM. 'Do you want me to fry?'

'The worms did,' said Ben heartlessly.

BBM shifted restlessly from foot to foot. I could see she was trying to think of a way to wriggle out of it. I gave her a very hard look and opened the hymn-book with emphasis. If I had to sing 'Abide with me', she could jolly well wear the black cape.

'Oh, all right!' she said resignedly and ambled back to the house.

Well, it didn't take us long to bury Fergus and for Mum to say a few words. Ben had decided we would have the hymn at the end of the service. By then I was getting into the mood of the thing and when I started to sing I got quite stuck into it. Mum joined in and Ben sniffled a bit. It's that sort of hymn, 'Abide with me' – very tear-jerking. And it made me think about Gran and what's going to happen to her when she dies. By verse three our voices were throbbing with emotion.

And that was when I suddenly became aware that we were being watched. And, of course, you know who it was watching us, don't you? You know who had rung the front door bell and then had come round the back, in case we were in the garden? You must have guessed what was going to happen long since. That's right. Standing at the corner of our house, dumb-struck with amazement, was none other than Chas Peterson. I nearly died. If the grave had been any bigger I would have crawled in there with Fergus, pronto. Instead, I stood there, mouth hanging open, and dropped the hymn-book in the hole instead.

BBM turned to see what the problem was. She, of course, wasn't fazed at all. She just carried right on singing until the very end and then bounded over to say hello.

'Sorry to interrupt,' said Chas, peering curiously over BBM's shoulder. 'Ben said to drop in sometime when I saw him at the fête.'

'Oh, that's fine,' said Mum breezily. 'Any time. We were just burying Fergus, our cat.'

'Oh,' said Chas. 'I'm sorry. Was he old?'

'Oh no,' she said brightly, and then she whisked him off to the kitchen while Ben filled in the grave and I hammered my brains out on the patio.

Chas, it transpires, has taken a liking to Ben. They have a lot of things in common – they both like computer games, *Asterix* books, cricket and, inevitably, cats. Chas's cat is expecting kittens. Ben's going to get first pick. Now isn't that nice? Excuse me while I just go and throw up somewhere – preferably down Ben's neck!

5

My Mum and
the Pig

Chas Peterson has spent a lot of time at our house over the last month. Not because of me, of course. No such luck. No, it's little brother Ben that he's interested in. I suppose they must have got talking for the first time that day in Oxford when I just had to see the shrunken heads again, and then there was the christening party and then the fête and then Chas stayed for tea after Fergus's funeral. Since then he seems to have been here nearly every other day! Incidentally, I could forgive Fergus a lot; at least he only left his hairs everywhere. Chas kept his promise about the kitten so now we have this cute little bundle of fluff frisking about the place, digging its cute little needle-sharp claws into everything, especially my legs. It's a good job it's too cold to wear shorts any more.

Anyway, Chas and Ben make an odd pair. Ben is short

and tubby and hopelessly scruffy, with this mop of hair about the colour and texture of damp straw – he won't let Dad get anywhere near it. Chas is tall and dark and tanned, with soulful brown eyes under mega-thick eyebrows. He looks sort of permanently thoughtful. He's not the totally immaculate type but at least he's always CLEAN. Ben seems to attract dirt. Of course Ben is still at junior school which makes it even more peculiar that Chas wants to be friends with him, but now that I really think about it, Chas is a bit of a loner. That's probably why I like him. I mean, I just can't be bothered with these macho types who do nothing but hang around in a great pack kicking a football about and swearing at each other – and there seem to be an awful lot of them at our school. Chas obviously isn't keen on them either – so I've had to get used to him drifting into our house and then drifting out again with Ben. Either that or they bury themselves in Ben's room for hours. I'm totally cool about it, of course. I just wait until the door is closed and then go and howl at the moon.

Well, one night last week, we were all sitting round the tea-table when Chas (he seems to eat with us rather a lot these days) suddenly asked BBM if we'd like to go round to his house for Sunday lunch.

'Mum told me to ask weeks ago, but I keep forgetting,' he added apologetically.

'Why, that'd be lovely!' said BBM enthusiastically, completely ignoring the face I was pulling. (Lunch with Mrs

Charming and Mr Bank Manager Peterson? I'd be bored out of my mind! I mean, Chas barely says a word to me! I'd just have to sit there for hours, being the polite daughter.)

'The only trouble is,' said Mum, 'that on Sundays we always have Gran here for the day.'

'Oh, that's all right,' said Chas. 'Mum knows that. She said she could come too.'

'Oh no, Mum,' I groaned, before I could stop myself. Before Gran got pneumonia we had taken her out to a restaurant on Dad's birthday. She came away with half the cutlery in her handbag. Ben rolled his eyes.

'Are you quite sure?' asked Mum. Even she looked a bit worried.

'Oh yes.' Chas nodded enthusiastically. 'Mum thought she might like a little walk round the farm. Would she be able to manage that?'

'The farm?' I broke in, rather rudely, I'll admit. 'I didn't know you lived on a farm.' I glared at Ben accusingly. 'You don't tell me anything, these days.'

Ben shrugged. 'He's always lived on a farm,' he said. 'His dad's an estate manager.'

'I thought he was a bank manager!' I said, and then remembered that I'd only assumed that because of how he'd looked at the christening. Of course, you wouldn't expect him to wear his wellies in church.

'Oh well,' said Chas, 'it doesn't matter, does it? Dad isn't really a farmer. He sorts out a lot of the finance and stuff, but the house we live in is the old Home Farm and we do keep pigs.'

'Pigs!' said Mum, excitedly. 'What sort?' My heart sank.

'Oh, all sorts,' said Chas. 'Dad's interested in rare breeds, so we've got a couple of Tamworths, a Gloucestershire Old Spot, an Oxfordshire Sandy and Black – oh, and a Vietnamese pot-bellied sow that's just had a litter. But that's not a rare breed, of course.'

'Of course,' said Mum knowledgeably, as if she knew everything there was to know about pigs. Perhaps hearing about the litter had gone to her head. She *had* gone a bit pink in the face and funny-looking. It was all too obvious that she'd set her heart on one of those pot-bellied piglets.

So what do you know? Sure enough, that very weekend off we all went to Mr and Mrs Pig-Loving Peterson's for Sunday lunch and a stroll round the farm. 'Bring your wellies,' said Chas. But I forgot.

'I can't believe it,' said BBM, as we stood in the little corridor which doubled as a boot-room, just inside the Petersons' back door. 'It was the last thing I said before we set off for church: "Don't forget your wellies."' She was seriously annoyed. It was just bad luck that I'd had new shoes only three weeks before for the start of the new school year or she probably wouldn't have been that bothered. It was even more bad luck that after two lovely weeks at the beginning of September, we'd had a fortnight of damp, miserable weather and quite heavy rain. It didn't look too promising for a walk actually. There were grey clouds gathering in the distance, even though it was quite bright and blustery for the moment.

I considered opting out of the farm tour. Dad had. He was going to Granny-sit. After behaving herself impeccably during the meal, she had settled herself in an armchair, slipped out her false teeth, put them in one of the decorative little pots which were arranged on a low-bookcase beside her and fallen asleep. Spending the afternoon with a snoring gran and a dad who wanted to read the Sunday papers wasn't exactly my idea of fun. I decided I'd rather see the pigs – and I'd rather make sure that BBM didn't buy one!

Fortunately, Mrs Charming came to my rescue. 'I'm sure we'll be able to find an old pair of boots that will fit,' she said soothingly. 'I tend to keep old wellingtons for just this sort of emergency.' She smiled brightly at Chas. 'Charles, perhaps you could take Kate over to the outhouse and have a look while the rest of us make a start? I'm sure some of us would like to burn off some energy. You can catch us up in a few minutes.' She looked meaningfully at Ben who was behaving a bit like a puppy who needs a good walk. Poor Ben. He's a bit on the clumsy side and it had been a huge strain for him to sit through four courses of polite conversation and delicate crockery. Then there was coffee in a sitting-room which looked like something from one of those posh magazines you find in dentists' waiting-rooms. (Question: do all dentists read posh magazines or do they buy them specially for the waiting-room?)

So that was how Chas and I came to find ourselves rummaging round the Petersons' outhouse for a pair of wellies for me. Considering how immaculate and well-organized the house was, I'd expected row upon row of neatly labelled boxes. Instead, the place looked like a bomb had hit it – or like whenever anything needed storing, someone just stood at the door and hurled it in.

Chas laughed when he saw my face. 'Mum keeps saying she'll sort it out one day,' he said, 'but she's been saying that since we moved here. I don't think she minds about the bits people can't see. I like it though. I come here a lot. And Ben likes it too.'

'I'll bet he does,' I said, with feeling. Ben is the world's worst hoarder. You can hardly get into his bedroom for the junk. I'd been wondering how Chas put up with it. Now I knew.

'Is that yours?' I asked, pointing to a battered armchair with no cover, across which was slung an old sleeping bag with two kittens snuggling inside. There was a coffee mug and a half-eaten packet of biscuits on one arm.

'Yes,' he said, and picked up the biscuits to offer me one. 'You'll probably think it's silly, but I come out here quite a lot to do my homework and to read. I prefer it to the house. And Mum doesn't want the kittens inside.' He tried to say it as if he couldn't care less what I thought, but he obviously did. I was flattered.

'I don't think it's silly at all,' I said. 'It's more lived in, out here.'

For a moment I thought I'd put my foot in it – I mean, his mother made the house how it was – but he wasn't bothered. He laughed again. He has a really nice laugh. 'You can say that again,' he said.

I smiled and picked up the book that was lying open on the chair.

Suddenly, his face changed. 'No!' he said urgently and made as if to snatch it from my hands. He stopped himself and blushed. I handed it back. It was *Little House on the Prairie* by Laura Ingalls Wilder – you know – the one that's been on the telly.

'I thought you only read *Asterix*,' I said.

He shrugged. 'Don't tell anyone,' he said. 'Please.'

'I won't,' I said. 'But why not? I really like those Little House books. They're not just for kids.'

He gave me the sort of look I'm always giving Ben; the sort which questions whether you've got any brain cells left. 'But you're a girl,' he said. 'Most of the boys at school think I'm a wimp anyway, just because I don't like football.'

'Well, most of the girls think you're cool,' I retorted, and then blushed myself.

'Really?' he said disbelievingly, but you could tell he was quite chuffed. 'Well, they wouldn't if they knew what I was reading. Boys are supposed to read horror, horror and nothing but horror.'

'Maybe that's why most boys are so boring,' I said firmly. (I only tell my parents I want to write horror stories to wind them up. Really I like anything but horror.) 'Anyway, hadn't we better find those wellies?' I wasn't quite sure I could cope with getting too deep and meaningful just yet. I was suddenly very aware that he was standing very close to me (well, there wasn't much floor space) and that had just been the most personal conversation we'd ever had.

It didn't take Chas long to find an ancient dustbin full of old wellies, but try as we might we couldn't find a matching pair which fitted me. There was one that was perfect; the others were all too big.

'Oh well,' I said, at last. 'I'll just have to wear odd ones. The others will be wondering what's happened to us.'

'Are you sure that's all right?' he asked. His mother had obviously drummed into him the importance of matching shoes and co-ordinated socks. I was beginning to see the advantage of Mum's more relaxed approach to life.

'I'm sure it won't kill me,' I said, trying not to laugh at his worried expression as I pulled the boots on. 'Come on.'

Chas led the way along an extremely muddy track. I had thought the pigs would be in a sty somewhere but they were out in the fields. I could see their corrugated metal arks in the distance when Chas pointed them out. We walked on in silence for a while. It was slightly up hill and quite hard work in the mud against the wind.

'Gran would never have managed this,' I said. 'Not since she's been ill. She wouldn't even manage a trip to Oxford now.' It was strange how suddenly I wasn't embarrassed to talk to him about that.

'No, she still seems quite poorly.'

I nodded. 'You're lucky your gran is so fit and well,' I said, remembering the powerful lady in the lilac suit.

'I don't know about that,' he grunted. 'She drives me mad.'

'Really? Why?' I asked, though I had a pretty good idea. She'd struck me as an interfering old bat.

'Oh, she's like Mum, only worse,' he said, with a shrug. 'Always on about what I'm wearing or how I'm doing at school or why I'm not in the cricket team when I'm so keen on cricket. At least your gran isn't always having a go at you. And if she did, your mum wouldn't agree! Your mum always seems to see the best in you. I never please anyone. Well, only Dad, anyway, and he never says much.'

I considered for a moment. He had a point. 'Yes, but Mum and Gran are a bit embarrassing,' I said, with a blush. 'And it's not easy having a mum who's a vicar.' It felt a bit disloyal actually putting it into words.

Chas snorted. 'So what? At least they're not always nagging you for not being how they think you ought to be. And they're not always worried about what other people think.'

'I don't think Gran notices other people any more,'

I said sadly. 'But I know what you mean about Mum. The trouble is, I wish she *did* care more what other people think. I nearly die every time she comes into school to do assembly or something.'

It was getting even harder to talk against the wind, so we walked on without speaking. I was thinking over what Chas had said about Gran and Mum and feeling more friendly towards them than I had done for months. I'd certainly rather have them than Mrs Charming Peterson and her mother. I wondered if Chas had to politely munch his way through a four-course lunch every Sunday. What a waste of time!

When we finally reached the pigs, Mum was leaning over the fence, scratching the back of Mrs Pot-belly enthusiastically. (She shouldn't really lean over fences with her figure.) Mr Pig-loving Peterson (who had been remarkably quiet over lunch) was chatting away to her animatedly. The signs didn't look good.

I sidled up to Ben who appeared to be having a man-to-pig chat with a massive hairy hog in the next pen. 'Has she said anything about buying one?' I hissed, out of the side of my mouth.

'Not yet,' said Ben. 'Why?'

'Oh, come on, Ben. You know Dad doesn't want her to have a pig and neither do I.'

'Oh, I wouldn't mind,' said Ben breezily. 'I think they're cute.'

'Of course they're cute!' I said, in exasperation, 'but that doesn't mean they'd be fun to have in our garden! Who d'you think'd be left to clear up the pig-poo? Not BBM, that's for sure!'

'Well,' said Mum, suddenly interrupting us. 'What d'you think? Shall we have one? We've plenty of room and we don't do much else with the space at the back.'

'No,' I said. 'Definitely not.'

'Why on earth not?' She was irrepressible. 'It'd eat all our left-over food, so it wouldn't be an extra expense. And if we had a sow we could try breeding them and then we could even make a profit.'

BBM is dreadful when she's got a project in mind. She gets all over-excited like a little kid. You could almost see dreams of podgy little porkers dancing before her eyes.

'Dream on, Mum,' said Ben appropriately. 'If you had a pig it would soon be sausages. Look what happened to the worms.'

'Yes, and remember that baby sparrow we almost reared – until you went and sat on it,' I added.

'It wasn't my fault it got out of its box!' BBM protested. 'How was I to know it was on the sofa?'

'And there was the playgroup hamster,' I went on relentlessly. 'Even that died the weekend we looked after it.'

'They only last a couple of years,' said Mum firmly. 'That was just bad luck.'

'And now Fergus is dead too,' added Ben, unjustly, I felt.

So did Mum. 'Hey, I'm not taking the blame for Fergus,' she retorted. 'He definitely wasn't my responsibility.'

But it was no good. We weren't going to be put off.

'Think of all the vet's bills,' Ben continued sombrely, shaking his head.

'And think of all the MESS!' I said. 'You'd never have time to clear it up. And think of the smell.'

'What smell?' demanded Mum. 'These pigs don't smell at all.'

'That's because we're standing halfway up a hill in a gale,' I said patiently. Really, when she's in this sort of mood, it's like trying to explain something to a child. She even begins to pout after a bit. Dad knows how to sort her out but Dad wasn't there. I dreaded to think what he would say if we didn't stop her somehow.

'Look,' I said crossly. 'You're always going on about how the Bible tells us to love our neighbour. Now will our next-door neighbours really like it if we keep a pig in our garden?'

'It would only be a little one,' said Mum, a bit peevishly. 'Why should it bother them?'

'I'd rather have a big one,' said Ben unhelpfully. 'I like the Oxfordshire Sandy and Blacks.'

'Oh, shut up, Ben,' I snapped. I was getting fed up with this conversation. I was cold, my wellies were rubbing and I did not want to go home with a pig. 'Whose side are you on?'

'I should think Mr Ponsonby would be delighted if I gave him some pig manure,' said Mum consideringly. 'It would be excellent for his roses.'

'Mum thinks horse manure is better,' said Chas, who I'd forgotten was listening to all this.

'Really?' said Mum. 'I should think pig manure would be just as good.'

That did it. I lost my temper. 'That's typical of you,' I shouted, stamping my foot in the mud. 'You're always going on about loving your neighbour but really you just want your own way. You just want to do what's nice for you! You don't care what I want or what Dad wants or what Mr Ponsonby wants – you just want a pig! And how would you find time to look after it? That's why the worms died. You couldn't even find time to read the instructions properly. I know exactly how it would end up. It'd be me and Ben who'd have to clean it out and chuck the muck over the fence for Mr Ponsonby. You're always getting someone else to do your dirty work for you. Look at Gran, stuck in that rotten nursing home. You can't even be bothered to look after her and if you do give her a day out you let her get into all sorts of trouble. If you want something to look after, why don't you stick her in a sty in the garden? And she'll probably die soon anyway, so you can't do any harm!'

Well, that's what I think I said. I certainly said that last bit. Terrible wasn't it? I'm awful when I get going. All the things I've half-thought for months come pouring out when I lose my temper. Of course, as soon as I'd said it, I turned on my heel and ran. I have a dim memory of all these open mouths and shocked faces, and then I was belting off down the hill as fast as I could.

Which was where I came unstuck. I was so busy being furious and getting away quickly that I wasn't watching where I was going and, of course, I had those odd wellies on too. Anyway, one minute I was stumbling along through the mud, and the next I was flat on my face, with pain like I'd never felt before throbbing up my left arm. I lifted my face a little to look and nearly threw up. My hand was lying at an angle which nature had never intended – almost as though it was a false one which hadn't been fitted quite right. I dragged myself into a sitting-position and fought back the tears. I looked back up the hill. No one had followed me. Mum had probably decided to leave me to calm down – and, to be honest, usually it's the best thing she can do. I struggled to my feet. The pain was unbelievable but settled down a bit once I was up. I felt very wobbly but I thought I could walk. After all, I was nearly back at the farmhouse. Then I did a really stupid thing. I'm not even quite sure why I did it. Maybe I wanted to get back at Mum or something – I don't know. Maybe I was just embarrassed about being quite so foul in front of the Petersons. Anyway, instead of going to the house and telling Dad what I'd done straight away, I wobbled over to the outhouse and hid.

I don't know how long I was in there before Chas came and found me. I don't expect the others hurried back from their walk; I mean, no one knew there was any need to. And then it would have taken a while for Chas to realize where I had gone. I was so dizzy and sick with the pain that it could have been hours or it could have been minutes. I don't like to think what Chas must have thought of me, going off in a sulk like that, and then, of course, when he found me, I just burst into tears. Typical! The first time we have a proper conversation and I go and cap it by behaving like a brat and a wimp!

'I've broken my wrist,' I blubbed, before he could say anything.

He stepped over the junk to take a look, as if he didn't believe me.

'Crikey,' he said, when he saw the damage. My arm and hand were now horribly swollen as well as the wrong shape. 'That's awful.'

'Stay right there,' he said, after a moment's thought and patted my shoulder gently. 'You don't look like you can walk. I'll get your dad.'

I won't tell you the details of the excruciating journey to the hospital or what the doctor had to say when he heard that I'd gone off and hidden – but I felt about half an inch tall when he'd finished. And don't let anyone kid you that it's fun to have a plaster cast – it's not! It's hot and it's heavy and it itches. I can't wait till they replace it with one of those fibreglass ones.

I'm having to type this very slowly and painfully with one hand – but it has kept me busy while I've been off school. And Mum hasn't bought a pig. We made it up, of course. We're not the sort of family to stay cross with each other for long.

'Tell me,' said Mum when I'd stopped snivelling all over her and she was tucking me into bed. 'Did you mean that bit about getting Gran out of the nursing home?'

'And putting her in a sty in the garden?' I asked, with a weak grin.

'You know what I mean,' said Mum firmly.

I fiddled awkwardly with my plaster cast. 'Well, only sort of,' I said. 'It just seems a bit mean for her to have to live there. I'd hate it.'

'I think she likes it actually,' said BBM. She must have seen the look on my face because she took my good hand and looked me straight in the eye. 'I am not trying to make excuses,' she said. 'I'm not perfect and the truth is I know I couldn't cope with your gran at home. Your dad agrees.'

'Couldn't you pray about it?' I said boldly.

BBM stood up. 'You think I haven't?'

She stood by the door for a minute before she switched off the light. 'I think, Kate,' she said quietly, 'that different people have different ways of loving their neighbours. But I promise I won't get a pig.'

I had to let it go at that. I really only said it because I was so cross. I mean, I've often thought how rotten it must be for Gran in that home but, to be honest, I couldn't cope with her here either. She's embarrassing enough as it is, whatever Chas might say. So, all in all, the only really awful bit is that when Chas patted my shoulder in that nice, concerned way, it was complete and total agony. And I've been stuck at home for two days and he hasn't even sent me a 'Get Well' card.

6

My Mum and
the Row

He came to see me! Chas actually came to see me! And he brought me some chocolates! Only a couple of hours after I'd been moaning about him not sending a 'Get Well' card! Well, the chocolates were from his mum really, but at least Chas brought them. And he talked – well, sort of – to me for about twenty minutes before Ben interrupted us.

I was in the sitting-room reading – that's one good thing about having a broken wrist, there's plenty of time to read – when BBM came in.

'Mind if I do my workout now?' she asked.

Her workout. That's the result of buying a bike. She's got fitness on the brain. And now that she's not allowed to have a pig, her new project is getting us all fit. It's a good job Mrs Charming Peterson fed us so well on Sunday because we haven't eaten properly since. BBM went to the library the next day and came home loaded with healthy-eating cookbooks and a workout video. If we'd still got the worms, she'd have fed our packet of Frosties to them; she tore up a perfectly decent half-loaf of white bread for the birds! It's been nothing but granary bread and lentils for two days. At least she hasn't gone and bought herself a leotard; she does the workout in psychedelic leggings and a baggy T-shirt. I suppose we have to be grateful for small mercies.

Anyway, in she bounced and put the video on while I studiously ignored her – or tried to. It's actually quite hard to get any sensible reading done when an apparition in electric pink leggings keeps flouncing past you and a relentless American voice keeps telling you to 'Burn!'

I'd just decided I'd better go to my room before I threw something at the TV, when the doorbell rang. I ignored it. It would either be some person from the church for Mum or it'd be Chas. And if it was Chas, he'd want to see Ben. So someone else could answer the door. All the same, my pulse fluttered a bit. After what happened on Sunday there was just a chance that Chas might pop his head in to say hello.

The door of the sitting-room opened. 'It's Chas,' said Dad, holding a hand to his eyes in mock horror. 'He wants to see Kate. Is it safe to let him in?'

I sat up and glared meaningfully at BBM.

'Oh, just ignore me,' she panted. By this time she was

lying on the floor with her legs in the air. 'I'll have finished in a minute.'

Chas stepped into the room nervously and hovered by the door. I'm not surprised. With BBM flinging herself backwards and forwards, you could get flattened if you stood in the wrong place.

He held out a box of chocolates. 'These are for you, Kate,' he said shyly. 'Mum sent them.'

I was just stammering a thank you when BBM sat bolt upright.

'Chocolates?' she said. 'Is that wise, Kate? Think of all the caffeine and the cholesterol and the calories. Perhaps you could have just one a day.'

Chas and I looked at each other awkwardly. The chocolates lay on the sofa between us. It was very difficult to know what to say. At that precise moment I could have throttled BBM. Who was she to go on about calories? Two workouts and a packet of lentils hadn't done much for her bum yet. She smiled at us serenely, then rolled over backwards and threw her legs in the air again.

Rrrriip! The electric pink leggings had had enough. I'm sure Jane Fonda would have been proud of the position BBM had got herself into, but right now the immediate challenge was how to get out of it while retaining a few shreds of decency. Chas's eyeballs were on stalks; I couldn't imagine Mrs Charming ever getting herself into a situation like this. Nine times out of ten there would have been something lying around – a grubby towel or a discarded sweater – that I could have tossed over to BBM in a moment. But there was nothing. For once the sitting-room was immaculate.

Wordlessly, I reached out my good hand for BBM to grab and then, scarlet to the roots of my hair, I hauled her to her feet. I wanted to die.

BBM, of course, didn't bat an eyelid. You'd think she made a habit of flaunting her knickers in public.

'Ah well,' she said, switching off the video. 'I suppose that's a sign that I should stop. Good excuse to buy some new leggings; I've had a lot of wear out of these.'

Then she strolled out of the room as if she hadn't a care in the world, while I felt like screwing myself up in a ball on the floor and chewing my fingernails off.

There was a difficult silence after she'd gone. I stared steadfastly at the chocolates, thinking that if I could just spit out a thank you, Chas would have a good excuse to go and find Ben.

Then Chas choked. I looked up. He was sucking in his cheeks hard and pulling the most grotesque face, while tears were rolling down his cheeks.

'I'm sorry,' he exploded. Obviously, the sight of my aghast face completely finished him off. He collapsed into an armchair and, clutching his stomach, he rolled around, helpless with laughter.

'But…' I said.

'Oh,' he moaned. 'It hurts. It hurts.'

Suddenly, I could see the funny side. Chas does have a very infectious laugh. I began to giggle, and, of course, once I'd started, I couldn't stop.

'Oh, I'll have to get a drink of water,' said Chas, struggling to his feet at last. 'I've got hiccups now.' He promptly let out a huge hiccup and, of course, that started us off again.

We staggered through to the kitchen. Chas splashed cold water in his face and I found him a clean glass. At that moment, Ben barged in. He must have just come down after finishing his homework.

'Oh,' he said, surprised. 'I didn't know you were here, Chas.'

'I just came with some chocolates for Kate,' he said, 'and then your mum…' He was beginning to shake again.

'Don't,' I groaned, elbowing him in the ribs. 'I ache all over.'

'I'm sorry,' he said and blew his nose hard. 'But your mum just cracks me up.'

Ben was looking at us as if we'd lost our marbles. Briefly, I told him what had happened.

'Uh,' he grunted. 'Doesn't sound such a big deal to me. Where are the chocolates?'

Typical Ben! Chocoholic or what?

'Still in the sitting-room,' I said. 'Go and get them if you want, before BBM feeds them to the kitten. She's decided that chocolate is unfit for human consumption this week.'

·I rooted around in the fridge for something more exciting than water to drink and Chas perched on the table. When Ben returned, we were chatting about our mothers' funny little ways.

'Well, go on, unwrap them,' I told Ben, barely breaking off from what I was saying. He did as he was told and then offered them round. We all munched happily until half the box was gone and then Ben said, 'Are you two going to rabbit on all night? I wanted to play Lemmings with Chas.'

Chas shook his head. 'Sorry, Ben. Can't tonight. I was only dropping by to give Kate the chocolates. I've got loads of homework to do. What are you doing tomorrow night?'

'I've got Cubs, remember? It's Thursday tomorrow.'

'And Friday's roller-skating,' added Chas.

'You could come round Saturday afternoon,' said Ben hopefully.

Chas shook his head again. 'Can't. Mum's taking me shopping. She says I need new clothes for the winter.'

'What about the evening?'

'I want to go to the cinema. Actually,' he said, turning to me, 'I wondered if you'd like to come too?'

I was just trying to get my breath back and wondering if this counted as 'being asked out by a boy' – when Ben piped up.

'Can I come too? What's the certificate?'

'Oh yes, I should think so,' said Chas hesitantly (and

I wasn't sure if he looked disappointed or not). 'It's only a PG.'

'So when are we going to play Lemmings?' Ben complained. 'It's more fun with two.'

'Sometime next week,' Chas promised, pulling on his jacket. 'I've got to go now or I'll never get all my homework done. See you soon.'

And the next minute he was gone.

I turned on Ben. 'Couldn't you keep your mouth shut, instead of inviting yourself along to the cinema with us, you rotten little squirt? Haven't you got any sense?'

Stupid thing to say! I knew it the moment I shut my mouth. Ben stared at me, jaw hanging open in amazement.

'You fancy him,' he said slowly, like someone emerging from a trance. 'You fancy Chas. That's why you were hanging around the kitchen with him, giggling like a drain. You fancy him.'

'So what if I do?' I snapped. 'Perhaps he fancies me too. Perhaps that's why he tried to invite me to the cinema.'

'Oh yeah! As if!' sneered Ben. 'That's why he said I could come too.'

'He didn't have much choice, did he?' I retorted icily.

'Well, if he was that keen, he should have waited till you were...' here he lowered his voice suggestively, 'alone together.'

I nearly hit him, but he had a point. It wasn't a point I wanted to admit, though.

'He probably thought you had more sense than to wade in with both feet,' I snapped. 'With friends like you, who needs enemies?'

'Oooh, hoity-toity!' said Ben maddeningly. 'You're just mad because he doesn't want to take you on his own.'

'No, I'm not!' I could have ripped out my tongue. I was so mad at giving myself away – especially when I wasn't at all sure what I felt any more. Ben was never going to let it drop – and he'd be watching Chas and me like a hawk from now on. It was the last thing I needed.

'Yes, you are. You're mad because you fancy him and he doesn't fancy you.'

Ben skipped sideways out of my reach and danced round to the other side of the kitchen table.

'Katie fancies Cha-as! Katie fancies Cha-as!' he chanted provocatively.

That did it. I lunged across the table and grabbed at him with my good arm. He shot out of my reach but skidded and fell sideways so the next minute I was on top of him, hitting, scratching, trying to grab him by his matted hair and bang his head on the floor.

At that moment, BBM walked in.

'What on earth…?' I heard her say and then, 'Kate! Ben! What are you thinking of? Stop it, this instant.'

I didn't, so she grabbed me by the collar and hauled me up. She's quite strong even if she's not very fit.

I was still fighting mad.

'Don't you dare say that again!' I shrieked at Ben. 'It's none of your business!'

'What isn't?' asked BBM calmly.

'Doesn't matter,' I mumbled and shot a warning glance at Ben. Either he didn't see it, or he was too worked up to pay any attention because he promptly spilled the beans.

'Kate fancies Chas and she thinks he fancies her,' Ben said.

'No, I don't!' I retorted. 'I just… oh, I don't know what I think!'

BBM looked at the half-eaten box of chocolates which still lay on the kitchen table. 'Maybe he does,' she said consideringly.

'No, he doesn't,' retorted Ben. 'Those chocolates are from his mum!' And he picked up the card that came with them and read:

Wishing you a speedy recovery
With our best wishes,
the Peterson family

'See? No love, no kisses, NOTHING!'

I knew all along who the chocolates were from, so I don't know what made me do it. Perhaps it was his triumphant grin which tipped me over the edge. Anyway, for the second time in less than a week, I completely lost my rag. Quick as a flash, I reached out across the table and slapped Ben hard across the face. Then I sat down at the table and howled. Much to my satisfaction, so did he.

At that moment, Dad came in from work.

'Having a nice day are we, dear?' he said to BBM. I could see where Ben gets it from.

Well, you don't do that sort of thing in our house if you know what's good for you. We were sent to our rooms to stew, while Mum and Dad got their heads together downstairs. That's always bad news – when they plan what they're going to say before they say it. But I knew all along we were really in for it, this time. They're very down on fighting and hitting, are our mum and dad. They have this favourite Bible verse which goes 'Do not repay evil with evil or insult with insult' and there's another one about offering your left cheek if someone hits you on the right cheek. I can see the sense in it – I mean, little fights can lead to big fights and big fights can lead to wars – but when Ben's being as irritating as he knows how, it's really hard not to give him a good going-over.

'Try praying about it,' said BBM coolly. 'You can't expect to do the really hard things without God's help.'

That's the trouble, I suppose. I'm not like Mum, chatting away to God all the time. I tend to just get on with life on my own and only pray when I feel like it. I suppose I'm not really giving God a proper chance.

'Well, if seeing Chas is going to make you behave like this, perhaps neither of you had better go to the cinema on Saturday,' said BBM when the lecture was over. My heart sank. We'd already lost two weeks' pocket money and been given extra chores to do.

'Ah, Mum!' whined Ben. 'That's not fair. She started it.'

'Ben!' said Dad, in a voice that made my insides quake. Ben kept quiet.

'But Mum,' I said, as politely as I could. 'It wouldn't be fair on Chas. He didn't want to go on his own. And it might not be on next week.'

Mum looked at Dad. Clearly, she wasn't sure what to say.

But Dad was. 'Well, if that's the case, perhaps he wouldn't mind if we all went together. Just so that we can keep an eye on you both.'

'That's a good idea,' said BBM brightly. 'I'm sure Chas won't mind. He's too young to be taking Kate out on her own, even if he does want to. We could take Gran too. She likes a good film and we haven't taken her to the cinema for ages.'

I groaned inwardly but I knew better than to say anything. There are times when I think BBM must be from another planet. Either that or it's just a big act she puts on. Too young to go out with someone when you're nearly thirteen! Huh! Surely BBM can't be that naive, even if she is a part-time vicar?

Ben caught my eye. 'Sorry,' he mouthed. 'You'd better be,' I mouthed back, but I gave him a wink too.

The chocolates were still lying on the table.

'Well, I don't think you'd better have any more of those,'

said BBM, sweeping them up. 'All that caffeine and those additives obviously did you no good whatsoever.'

'I'll look after them,' said Dad, calmly taking them out of her hand. 'I'll keep them until we think Kate and Ben deserve them.'

BBM let out a sort of whimper.

'Now don't look like that, dear,' he said sweetly, and kissed her on the cheek. 'You won't be needing them, remember? You're on a fitness campaign.'

7

My Mum and the Cinema Trip

Well, we didn't go to the cinema the Saturday after I broke my wrist. No, it wasn't because Chas refused point blank to be seen in a public place with my family (though I could understand it if he did!). It was because he went down with CHICKENPOX! Of all the things to go and catch! I thought everyone had that when they were five-and-a-half! It turns out that it's one of those things you ought to get when you're little because it's much worse when you're older. Poor Chas was really ill with it. He was off school for over two weeks and he still looks a bit poxy even now. He nearly went demented with boredom too – because he even had spots in his eyes. He couldn't read or watch TV for a week, let alone use the computer. Thank goodness you hardly ever get chickenpox twice. I'd go mad if I couldn't type, now that I take out all my feelings on this keyboard!

I missed Chas. I'd got used to him hanging around our house, even if he did spend most of his time with Ben. And I'd been looking forward to getting to know him better now that we'd broken the ice. We timed it really well: I went back to school with my arm in plaster and he promptly stayed home with the pox. He's never had much to say to me at school, so I was surprised how much I missed his friendly face around the place.

I don't know whether it's because of Mum being the local vicar (and that means she turns up in school for assemblies and a few other things) but I can't say I'm overwhelmed with really close friends. There's a gang of girls that I hang around with and we get on all right but I haven't really got a 'best friend'. I'm not a complete outcast or anything like that – I just haven't got anybody who's that special. Most of the boys are complete nerds and either ignore the girls completely or are out to show how macho they can be (and most of the girls are just desperate to attract their attention). And I seem to be the odd one out. A bit like Chas really. I read a lot and make up stories and quite like sport – and none of the girls are really into any of that, except for posing on the tennis courts in the summer. I don't even know that I really want a boyfriend or if I fancy Chas – it's just that he's always struck me as being someone I might get on with, given half a chance. And he is nice to look at too!

Oh dear, I don't know. It's very confusing. I've really

been trying to think it through while Chas has been off school. I mean, when we were looking for the wellies that day in Chas's outhouse, I did feel quite peculiar, being alone with him and so close – but I don't think I want to get into all that boyfriend/girlfriend stuff yet. I thought I did – I mean, everyone else my age seems to – but what I think I really want is a proper friend – boy or girl, I don't care. And I'd hate to go out with Chas for a few weeks and then split up and have him never speak to me again. Because that's what seems to happen. I know loads of kids who are all lovey-dovey for a few weeks and spend the next six months slagging each other off. Yuk!

The irritating thing is that BBM has gone completely paranoid about Chas and me. It's all Ben's fault, of course. If he hadn't gone and told BBM that I fancied Chas, she'd be none the wiser – and we wouldn't have just survived the most embarrassing trip to the cinema I've ever had in my life.

BBM wouldn't let Ben or me visit Chas while he was really ill.

'There's no point,' she said, when Ben asked. 'He's not well enough to enjoy visitors. And I know it's unlikely that you'd catch chickenpox again, but there's always a slight risk. And I don't want to nurse you both through that again. It was bad enough the first time. Wait till he's getting better.'

And then, a few days later, when I asked, she was still

remarkably cagey. 'Just give it a few more days,' she said. 'He's still infectious till the spots have scabbed over.'

In the end he rang us.

'Please come and see me,' he begged. 'I'm so bored I shall start picking my scabs off soon.'

BBM wasn't easy to convince. 'Well, how are you going to get there?' she demanded. 'We've only got one car now.'

'He says his mum will get us,' I said. 'And bring us back.'

'But she can't go to all that trouble. She's got enough to do with Chas being ill.'

'He says she'd be glad to,' countered Ben. 'He's getting on her nerves.'

'What's wrong with us going on our bikes, anyway?' I enquired. 'He's often gone home from here by bike.'

'I don't like the idea of you cycling out there on your own,' said BBM. 'It's very isolated.'

Ben stared. 'But we went all over the place in the summer,' he said. 'You weren't bothered then.'

'That was the summer,' said BBM. 'The nights are drawing in now.'

This was all so unlike BBM that I began to smell a rat. I suddenly remembered what she'd said when the cinema trip was first mentioned – that I was too young for Chas to take me out alone. So that was what all this was about! Well, who'd have thought it? And BBM is usually so open about what she thinks. I was shocked. And it made me cross too. I mean, what does she take me for? Doesn't she trust me?

Well, two can play at that game, I thought. No way was I going to put her out of her misery if she wasn't going to be honest with me!

'I thought there was a bit in the Bible about visiting people when they're ill?' I said innocently.

'Which bit d'you mean?' BBM asked suspiciously.

'Oh, you know, where Jesus says that if you visit someone who's sick, it's as if you'd visited him when he was sick. I thought that meant we were *supposed* to visit sick people.'

'Ye-e-s,' said BBM slowly. I thought I'd got her there. It wasn't going to be easy to come up with an answer to that. But BBM has an answer to everything, even if it's only 'I don't know.'

'Thank you for pointing that out, Kate,' she said, after a moment's thought. 'You're quite right, of course. I think the only answer is to arrange for your dad to get a lift home from work. Then I can pick you both up after school and we'll all go together. I really should have thought of visiting Chas myself earlier. It's been very remiss of me.'

Touché. My heart sank. Surely she wasn't thinking of hanging around with us for a couple of hours to make sure we didn't misbehave? This was awful! Surely she wasn't going to turn into a sort of middle-aged minder, as well as embarrassing me at every opportunity? I groaned inwardly. With BBM, anything is possible.

Thank goodness for Dad, that's all I can say. He really has

got the knack of dragging her back when she's gone off the deep end.

'Can't Mrs Peterson get them and bring them back?' he asked at teatime, when BBM told him she was planning to borrow the car.

'Oh, we don't want to put her out,' said Mum firmly.

'Rubbish!' said Dad, even more firmly. 'It's only three miles. It wouldn't put her out at all. Far less than it will Greg if he has to give me a lift home.'

'But I thought I ought to visit Chas too,' said BBM rebelliously.

'What on earth for?' said Dad, eyeing her as if she was mildly deranged. 'Are you into *Asterix* and cricket all of a sudden or something?'

'No, but it is part of my job to visit the sick.'

'The sick with chickenpox?!' Dad gave Mum a very odd look. 'Are you out of your mind? Are you going to visit every spotty toddler in town? What's all this about? For heaven's sake, leave poor Chas in peace. He didn't ring you and beg you to go round. I'll go and pick up Kate and Ben later in the evening if you're really worried about putting Mrs Peterson out.'

BBM didn't say anything else. It was getting dangerously close to a row and, as a rule, they don't argue in front of us. BBM slammed around with the pans a bit and Dad dolloped the food out with rather more gusto than usual but that was the end of the matter as far as we were concerned. We went to see Chas on our own.

Poor Chas! He really had been suffering. He was all pale and peaky looking and very, very spotty. But it was great to see him. All that laughing we did together after BBM's leggings split really seems to have broken the ice. It was as if we'd been friends for ages. Ben whinged a bit about us jawing on, so we played Monopoly together to keep him happy. In a way it was a pity Mum hadn't come; she'd have seen there was nothing to worry about. I just hope Chas doesn't go and ask me out. I wouldn't know what on earth to say.

Chas's mum took us home in the end and it was obvious from the moment we walked into the kitchen that Mum and Dad had been 'having a talk'. Mum's eyes were a bit too bright and her cheeks were flushed.

'Had a nice time?' she asked casually. 'Is Chas feeling better?'

'Yes,' I said. 'But he looks awful so he's not going to go back to school till next week. Can we go and see him again tomorrow?'

'It's a bit much to expect Mrs Peterson to give you your tea two days running,' said BBM, bristling immediately.

'But…' I began. I wanted to say that Chas had eaten endless teas at our house.

Dad cut me short. 'How about the next night?' he asked calmly. 'Won't you have homework to catch up with tomorrow night?'

I nodded.

'Well, that's settled then,' said Dad briskly. 'Glad to hear he's on the mend. He's a nice lad. Oh, and your mum wondered whether he'd like to come with us to the cinema when he's properly better. That Spielberg film he wanted to see looks like it'll run for weeks yet. What d'you think? We could go to celebrate your plaster coming off next week.'

There was the sort of twitch to Dad's face that made me think he was dying to laugh – but that's the great thing about Dad. I'm sure there are times when he thinks BBM is completely out of her tree (don't we all?) but he never, ever laughs at her. When I grow up, that's the sort of man I'd like to marry. One who's on my side. A real friend.

'Well, we could ask him,' I said dubiously. I wasn't too keen on the idea myself. It was a bit like inviting someone out for an evening with the Addams Family. And I knew very well what BBM was up to. She just wanted to stop Chas from inviting me out alone.

'Well, go on then,' said Dad. 'Only when you do, try not to look as though the very idea is enough to make you throw up.'

So I asked Chas. And he said yes. He seems immune to the fear of public humiliation. Maybe the fact that we were paying helped. Despite what he says about BBM and Gran, I can't believe any normal person would choose to be seen in public with my family of their own free will. At least

I don't feel uncomfortable being seen with Dad any more, now that ponytails and earrings are fashionable for men. He can always be relied on to behave himself too. But BBM? And Gran? They ought to carry a public nuisance warning!

The trouble started before we'd even got into the cinema; we were only in the queue. Anyone would have thought we were the Royal Family on walkabout, the amount of waving and smiling that was going on. Dad, of course, knows half the town's population from his salon and BBM knows the other half from… well, who knows? All her crazy projects, I suppose. And being a general busybody. I thought we'd never get our tickets, the number of times BBM announced that she must just go and speak to Mrs Whoever-it-happened-to-be because she hadn't seen her for months. Which makes you wonder what she *has* been doing all those times she's supposed to have been visiting the people who live near the church.

We finally got to our places, once we'd disentangled Gran's net shopping bag (don't ask me what she was doing with that on a trip to the cinema) from the studded leather jacket of the man in front of her. He was very charming and apologetic until she'd got free and was heading off up the stairs. 'What a very helpful young lady that was,' she announced blithely and very audibly to the world in general. OK, so he'd got long hair, but you'd think that the three-day stubble might have given her a clue. You could see him wishing he'd strangled her with her string bag.

'Stupid old geezer,' he snarled.

She waved and gave him a regal smile.

Once we were in our seats everything went well for a few short minutes. Then someone tapped Gran on the shoulder.

'Excuse me,' said a very polite voice from behind. 'Would you mind removing your hat? I'm having difficulty seeing the screen.'

Gran turned and gave the woman a look that would have reduced Arnold Schwarzenegger to a pulp.

'No, I certainly cannot,' she said coldly. 'There is a nasty draught in here.'

As the rest of us were all peeling off as many layers as was decent because the auditorium was very stuffy and extremely full, this seemed a touch unreasonable. Both Mum and Dad decided to muscle in.

'I'm extremely sorry,' said BBM, turning to the woman and smiling sweetly. 'She is quite attached to her hat.'

Dad, meanwhile, was trying to unobtrusively remove Gran's hat while explaining very patiently that it was getting in the way.

'No,' she said firmly and hung onto it for grim death.

'Now, Mother...' Dad started and tried to prise her fingers away.

'No,' Gran shouted. 'I want my hat!'

By this time the lights were going down. People were beginning to look in our direction and say, 'Shh!' I'd already spotted quite a few girls from our school and I was pretty sure they'd noticed us.

'Why on earth did we bring her?' I groaned.

'Don't be mean,' said Ben. 'She loves the cinema. It probably reminds her of going out with Grandad. And she really likes Spielberg. She gets quite excited.'

'That's what I'm afraid of,' I said. 'If it's anything like the Jurassic Park films she'll probably have a heart attack.'

'No she won't, stupid,' retorted Ben. 'She's tougher than you think. That's what the doctor said after she had pneumonia.'

By this stage, the argument over the hat had developed into a polite tug of war. Dad was still pulling at the hat and Gran was still hanging on for grim death, her hands clamped firmly over her ears. Why BBM was still reciting twenty different reasons for removing your hat in a cinema is anybody's guess. Gran's protests were becoming louder and louder and finally she completely lost her patience. She stood up abruptly and announced in a loud, clear voice, 'I have put my hat on and I will keep it on. Thank you.'

'Shhh!' said everyone within twenty paces, turning round to give us all a good hard stare. There was a fair amount of tut-tutting too. If this goes on much longer they'll be arrested for granny-bashing, I thought miserably. It was a good job it was still only the adverts, or I think we'd have been chucked out of the cinema.

The lady in the row behind tapped Mum on the

shoulder. 'Please don't worry,' she said apologetically. 'If I swap places with my husband, I'm sure I'll be able to see perfectly.'

I heard BBM's sharp intake of breath. 'Turn the other cheek,' I thought mischievously, thinking that if I'd been in Mum's position I'd have been extremely rude. I mean, why hadn't the silly woman suggested that five minutes ago? Mum, of course, rose to the occasion. 'Thank you,' she said, in a perfectly normal voice. 'That would be extremely helpful.'

Peace reigned for a few moments, but I might have known it wouldn't last. 'Are we going to have an ice cream?' enquired Gran. in a voice loud enough to drown the adverts. 'I always have an ice cream when I go to the pictures. Are you short of money or someting?'

Every eye in the place seemed to turn in our direction. I distinctly saw two particularly bitchy girls from another class in my year staring at us and sniggering.

They sniggered even more a few minutes later. Mum and Dad gave in gracefully. They decided we could all have lollies or ice creams.

'But Mother had better only have a tub,' said Dad firmly. 'She ought to be safe with that.'

'Can I have a Feast?' pleaded Ben. 'Please? I haven't had one for ages.'

'That's because the last time you had one you were sick,' said BBM dubiously.

'Aw, Mum,' Ben protested. 'That was only because it was at the fair and I went on the Waltzers straight afterwards.'

'Hmm…' said Mum. 'I'm not so sure.'

'You'd better hurry,' said Dad, 'or you won't get anything. The film'll start in a minute.'

'Come on, Ben,' said Mum. 'I can't carry everything myself.'

Well, I don't know what happened on the way back. Perhaps BBM was hurrying – or perhaps she tripped over someone's foot. Anyway, whatever it was, one minute BBM was hurrying down the steps towards us and the next minute there was this almighty crash and she was lying spread-eagled on the stairs. The ice creams she'd been carrying shot off in three different directions. It was a pity she'd already taken the top off a Cornetto and started licking it, because that landed sticky end down in a rather smart gentleman's lap.

Chas fell about laughing. I just wanted to die.

BBM struggled awkwardly to her feet and we could see her apologizing profusely to all and sundry before the lights finally went down.

'I'm glad I didn't let her carry my Feast,' whispered Ben unsympathetically, when he got back to his seat. Honestly! That boy! All he thinks about is chocolate!

BBM staged a rapid recovery. Rather too rapid, in fact. Only a few minutes later she was off to tell a rather rowdy bunch of kids (from our school, of course) to keep quiet or she would get the manager. I nearly walked out and went home.

'My mum's always doing that,' whispered Chas sympathetically. 'Awful, isn't it?'

I grinned at him, even though he couldn't see me. It had just been getting a little bit irritating, the way he couldn't seem to see any problem with BBM.

We were well into the film before the next disaster struck. It was a particularly tense moment when Gran suddenly let out a sort of strangled, gargling noise.

That's it, I thought. She's having a heart attack. Why, oh why, did we bring her?

She wasn't – but I didn't know that until later. All I knew was that she appeared to be choking to death and Dad and Mum were bundling her out of her seat and along the row as fast as they possibly could. Of course, like me, all the people in the way assumed it was an emergency and there was a frantic commotion as they scrambled out of the way. A few rows away another man saw what was happening and started scrambling out too.

'Excuse me. I'm a doctor,' we could hear him saying, over and over again.

'Better stay here,' said Chas, grabbing my arm as I leaped up to follow Mum and Dad. 'You'd only be in the way.'

I sat down with a bump, but I'd lost track of the film. All I could think of was what might be happening to Gran.

And then, just a few minutes later, they all came back. Gran saw me craning round anxiously and gave me a cheery wave through the gloom. Then the whole performance of getting her back to her seat began. I put my arms over my head and tried to pretend I wasn't there.

Chas elbowed me in the ribs. 'Cheer up,' he whispered. 'At least she isn't dead.'

'No, but I wish I was,' I moaned.

'What was wrong?' I demanded, in a stage whisper, when Mum, Dad and Gran were all safely sitting down again.

'Dentures stuck together with a wine gum,' hissed Dad. 'Here.' He passed me a small bag. 'You and the others might as well share them out. Don't tell your mum.'

Wine gums! I ask you. What will she do next?

'But what was she doing with a bag of wine gums?' I demanded, on the way home.

'Oh, it's my fault,' said Dad. 'I should have thought. We always had wine gums at the cinema when I was a kid – but it beats me where she got them from.'

But that was later. Meanwhile we watched the rest of the film – and reached the end without further trouble – apart from Gran letting out regular whoops of excitement and cheering on the good guys rather too enthusiastically.

'That was great! Thanks very much,' said Chas to Mum and Dad as we shuffled our way out at the end.

'Yeah, thanks,' I said glumly. I was only too aware of all the kids from our school, nudging and pointing and exchanging remarks. Perhaps Chas needs glasses.

Ben was slow to follow us.

'You all right?' I asked, waiting for him.

'I don't feel very well,' he said limply. 'I think Mum was right about that Feast.'

There was a crush by the door. There was no way he was going to get out of there quickly. I looked round frantically but it was just as bad by all the other exits.

'Enjoy the film, did you?' interrupted a sarcastic voice from just behind me. 'You and Chas?'

It was one of the bitchy girls from our year. Her name's Lisa.

I opened and shut my mouth a couple of times, desperately trying to think of some cutting reply but at that moment Ben said, 'I'm going to be...' and, lurching forwards, he threw up spectacularly.

Moving while you're throwing up is not a good idea. It increases the damage. On this occasion, however, I secretly thought Ben had done rather well. Most of the mess was on the carpet but he'd also managed to splatter Lisa's coat.

'That'll teach her,' I gloated. I think BBM's got some more work to do on me. I'll never get to heaven at this rate.

8

My Mum Goes
to the Park

Today started well. BBM was in good form at church. She'd got someone to do a Bible story puppet show and she'd taken along her collection of shakers and bells and hooters so all the kids who can't read had something to play during the songs. When it was time to pray, she asked everyone to call out things they wanted to pray for, while she wrote them up on a big screen. Then we all had to be quiet for a few minutes and pray about something. I like it when Mum does something like that. I mean, I'm not very sure about this praying business – I never seem to find time to do it, for one thing – but when I'm forced to pray, I quite enjoy it. Mum says a lot of people think you've got to use special words when you're praying, but really it's just like talking to a very good friend. I think it's even easier than that because you haven't even got to get the words exactly right. It's more as if someone kind and understanding is just listening to your thoughts. So I had a good think and hoped it was going to work. Because I needed a bit of help.

It was the business with Chas. By the time I'd written all that stuff about the cinema last night, I reckoned I'd made up my mind. Chas is my friend. OK, he's a boy and he's just about the best friend I've ever had but he's just a friend – so BBM can jolly well stop all the top security minder bit. But then, when I was lying in bed trying to get to sleep, I couldn't stop thinking about him. I even started wondering what it would be like if he kissed me. It's all very confusing. One minute I can feel my heart beating faster, just because I'm thinking about him, and the next minute I'm sure that if he kissed me I'd curl up and die of embarrassment. Maybe it's just because BBM is being so paranoid. I've even started thinking that some of the other boys in our class aren't bad looking. I can't believe it. I mean, two years ago, they were all just scabby little oiks who thought it was a big thrill to flick snot-balls! Gross! What's wrong with me?

Anyway, enough of all that. This afternoon was beautiful – wonderfully sunny and bright for late autumn and a real change after all the rain we've been having. I decided to get my bike out and go for a spin round the park. I haven't been out on it since my plaster came off. I wanted a bit more time to think. Ben didn't want to come, fortunately. I wasn't in the mood for his never-ending stream of chatter – I just wanted to go off on my own.

I was surprised how quiet the park was, but then I suppose it was quite chilly. I could feel the cold air catching in the back of my throat as I cycled along – not the sort of weather for hanging around the playground with little kids, especially with all the puddles and mud. It was great for me, though. I suppose you could even call it an adventure playground, if you were being generous. There are a couple of enormous slides and one of those aerial runways – you know, the sort of thing where you jump off a ramp while clinging onto some sort of handle on a pulley and you go whizzing along this cable until you hit the ramp at the other side – unless you fall off in the middle, of course! There's a brilliant climbing-net which is shaped like a pyramid, and a trampoline set into the ground so you can't fall off. Well, I know I'd gone out for a quiet think but I'm afraid I couldn't resist the temptation to try everything out a few times while there was hardly anyone around to get in the way.

Unfortunately, after only a few goes on the aerial runway, my wrist began to hurt and before very much longer I decided that if I threw myself down the slide one more time, I'd be sick. I wasn't ready to go home though so I strolled over to one of the swings. I love just swinging gently, trailing my toes on the ground and letting the world go by. It's a great way to rearrange your brain.

So I was lost in thought when I heard my name called. Well, at first I didn't even realize it was me that was being called.

'Kat-ie. Kat-ie.' It was more of a chant than a call. I hate being called Katie. It sounds so twee and little girlish. Ben always calls me Katie when he wants to wind me up. So it took me a while to work out that the voice – well, voices, actually – were speaking to me.

Their owners were quite close when I finally looked up, and approaching quickly. Oh no! They were the girls from the cinema – the very last people I wanted to meet. After that perfectly timed performance by Ben, the whole business of getting Lisa's coat cleaned up had been hideously embarrassing. Her name's Lisa, by the way. Mum asked her. Funny, I've never liked anyone called Lisa. Her friend's called Donna.

So what did they want with me? They didn't exactly look friendly. I'm not saying I was scared – that would have been too strong a word for it – but there was a distinctly wobbly feeling in my tummy. If I hadn't left my bike on the other side of the playground, I would have gone – quickly. As it was, I was cornered.

'Hiya, Katie,' said Lisa, with an unpleasant smile. 'Having a nice swing?'

'Yes thanks,' I replied, as brightly as I could manage.

'Is your brother going to buy me a new coat then?' she asked casually, but coming very close to where I was sitting.

'I thought Mum helped you to clean it up all right,' I said nervously. I didn't like the way she was standing over me.

'It still stinks,' she said, with a toss of her head.

I tried to remember what Mum had said to Chas's grandma when she'd been so cross after the christening, but my mind had gone completely blank. Donna had closed in on me now too. I was conscious of my knuckles looking very shiny and white as I gripped the chains of the swing extremely hard. There was something very frightening about having those two hostile faces sneering down at me.

I gave myself a mental shake. Don't be so stupid, I told myself. They've hardly even said anything. They can't do much to you in broad daylight in a public park. I tried very hard to ignore the fact that there was hardly a soul in sight.

'I'm sure it'll be all right after it's been in the washing-machine,' I said, in what I hoped was a firm and confident voice.

'Oh, listen to her,' Lisa mocked. 'I'm sure it'll be all right after it's been in the washing-machine. It was brand new, that coat was.'

My brain reeled. Was I being stupid? Was there really something wrong with suggesting she put it in the washing-machine? Or were they just out to get me, whatever I said? And if so, why? Until yesterday, I'd never had anything much to do with them – I just knew them by reputation. Why were they suddenly picking on me? I was scared – well, terrified, actually. It was awful to feel so alone and trapped and helpless. I've never been bullied at school. Nobody's ever gone deliberately out of their way to make my life a misery – but unless I thought of some way out of this, it looked like these two were about to start. I was already worrying about what they might do to me at school. I knew what Mum would say. 'Pray,' she'd say. 'Just pray.' So I did. Silently. Help! I prayed. Help!

Donna was looking bored. 'So where's Charlie-boy?' she asked tauntingly. 'Stood you up, has he? That why you're sitting here all on your own?'

I didn't answer. I was trying to work out what to do. If someone's decided to pick on you, it's no good letting them think you're just going to take it. But apart from thumping them, I couldn't think what else to try.

'Can't see what you see in him,' she continued disdainfully. 'He's a complete drip.'

Now, I might be confused about how I feel about Chas. And I did feel as if my guts had turned to jelly. But I do have a certain amount of loyalty. And I wasn't going to sit around listening to Chas being called a complete drip. Maybe anger inspired me. Maybe God answered my prayer. Who knows? Whatever it was, I suddenly remembered a trick I'd perfected a couple of years ago and which Ben hasn't managed yet. The trick is to get the swing moving from sitting without putting your feet on the ground. What you do is jump up so you're standing on the swing (it nearly pulls your arms out of your sockets, by the way) and at the same time give this almighty push forwards with your knees bent. With any luck, the swing goes shooting up into the air and you're away. I didn't stop to think. I just did it. They dived out of my way.

'You're just jealous,' I told them, as they sprawled in the dirt. They were lucky – and I suppose I was too. If they'd moved any slower, they could have been in the hospital and I could have been in serious trouble. As it was, a searing pain had shot through my poor abused wrist and I had to bite my lip hard to stop myself from crying out.

'Urgh! Look at the state of my jacket!' shouted Lisa furiously, as she brushed herself down. 'And my jeans are filthy too.'

Donna didn't say anything. She just looked evil. I was very glad I was out of reach.

Just then, from my position high above their heads, I spotted something I couldn't quite believe.

'You can go and tell my mum, if you like,' I told them triumphantly, my sore wrist forgotten. 'She's just over there.' I jerked my head in the right direction. I didn't mention that Chas was with her, but they could see perfectly well.

'I'm going to get you for this,' said Lisa, with a snarl.

'Oh yeah?' I retorted, safe on my airborne perch and with BBM and Chas rapidly approaching on bicycles. 'You and whose army?'

She narrowed her eyes at me and turned on her heel.

'You wait,' she tossed over her shoulder. 'Just you wait.'

They walked off across the play area and through the

little gate that stops the dogs from coming in. I watched them anxiously as they made their way round the duck pond, heads together, deep in conversation. Now that the adrenalin was wearing off, I felt scared again. What were they plotting? Or would they decide to leave me alone? Had I proved that I wasn't such a soft touch after all?

My thoughts were cut off abruptly. 'Watch out!' I yelled, pointlessly, to Mum. She was too far away and it was too late.

There's an ornamental bridge over the stream that feeds the duck pond. It's a neat little hump and the path twists immediately after it. It's perfectly passable on a bike, providing you're careful. It's not so easy when the path is wet and muddy, especially when you've got a figure like BBM's! And she wasn't prepared for it. She was going too fast and, as she tried to adjust for the twist in the path, her back wheel slid from under her – just as my two tormentors arrived at the bridge. Even from where I was, I could see the great shower of mud and water splattering the two girls as the bike slewed round and landed at their feet. BBM, meanwhile, was catapulted off the bike and bellyflopped – splash! – straight into the pond. I leaped off the swing in mid-flight and raced across the play area. Bullies or no bullies, I couldn't just leave Chas on his own to confront the two furious girls and rescue BBM who, plastered in pondweed and mud, was now terrifying the wildlife!

'Is my bike all right?' demanded BBM, before we'd even hauled her out of the water.

'Looks fine to me,' said Chas. 'You were lucky.'

'Lucky?' BBM exploded. 'I'm soaking wet and freezing cold and you think I'm lucky?'

She grabbed our hands and scrambled up the bank. It took a while. It was all wet, slippery clay and really steep. I was ready to drop when we'd finally beached her.

She stood up, spat out some weed, wiped her face (which merely added more mud to what was already there) and scowled at Donna and Lisa who were still hanging around, sniggering. I suppose their soaking had faded into insignificance, compared with Mum's.

'And what do you think you're laughing at?' BBM snapped at them, apparently unaware that she ought to be making an apology. 'Have you nothing better to do than stand around, laughing at other people's misfortunes?'

I wanted to die. Nails in my coffin, I thought to myself, despairingly. This scene wasn't exactly going to add to my popularity with them now, was it?

'Come on, Mum,' I said. 'I think we'd better go home.'

'Really?' said Mum sarcastically. 'Actually, I fancied a go on the swings.'

I blushed uncomfortably. She clearly wasn't seeing the funny side of this little escapade. But she didn't need to treat me like an idiot in front of Chas – or Donna and Lisa.

Lisa and Donna had turned to go. 'See you tomorrow then, Katie,' said Lisa sweetly. 'Sorry we can't stay to help.' But the look on her face meant trouble, I was sure.

'Come on,' said Chas awkwardly. 'Want to borrow my jacket?'

'It wouldn't fit me,' BBM said testily. She thought for a moment. 'I think I'd better run to the phone booth by the gates and ring for a lift home,' she decided. 'Can you bring my bike?'

'Sure,' said Chas. We watched her jog off down the path. She'd barely gone a hundred yards when we saw her wave at a couple who were chasing after their dog.

'She'll be all right,' I said grumpily. 'She probably met that pair on an abseiling course. Any minute now, he'll give her his coat and offer her a lift home. You watch.'

I was right. Moments later, BBM was wearing the man's anorak and the poor dog was back on its lead.

'She met them on an abseiling course?' said Chas, in a tone of disbelief.

'It's a long story,' I said wearily. 'Now how are we going to get three bikes home? Mine's over by the trampoline.'

'Easy,' said Chas. 'I can ride and push at the same time. But why do we have to go now? Your mum said you were down at the park, so I thought I'd come too.'

'And she came with you?'

'Yeah. Said she could do with a breath of fresh air.'

'Oh,' I said. I glanced at his face quickly. He didn't look as if he thought there was anything odd about Mum coming with him. I decided I wouldn't say anything about it. It would only complicate things.

'Come on,' he said. 'Let's go on the runway. It'll start getting dark soon. I'll race you over.'

We had a great time on that aerial runway. We tried pushing each other off the ramp, dragging each other along, both hanging on at the same time – you name it. When my wrist couldn't take any more, we raced each other on the slides and then we tried out the trampoline. Chas made me crack up by giving this mock Olympic commentary on every move I made. In the end, we both collapsed on the canvas, exhausted. I examined my wrist a little anxiously – it was throbbing a bit.

'We'd better go,' I said, when I'd got my breath back and decided my wrist was OK. 'The gates close at dusk.'

Chas lay where he was. 'Kate,' he said, in a quiet, tentative voice.

Oh no! I thought, panic-stricken. He's going to ask me out! What on earth shall I say?

But he didn't.

'Those girls,' he said awkwardly. 'Donna and Lisa. Had they been having a go at you?'

'It was nothing,' I lied. How did he know? Now that they'd gone, I felt really silly about it. I mean they hadn't done anything to me, had they? And I couldn't possibly tell him what they'd said. Or I didn't think I could.

'I just wondered,' he said, sitting up. 'Only…'

'What?' I demanded curiously. I could see him blushing in the gloomy light.

'Well, Lisa fancies me,' he said, refusing to look at me. 'She's always sending me notes. And Donna's tried to persuade me to go out with Lisa a couple of times. I just thought… well, you know… they can be really nasty…' His voice trailed away in embarrassment.

'Huh!' I snorted. So that was it! The two-faced toads! I couldn't believe it. I bounced to my feet and offered him a hand up. I was suddenly filled with the urge to do battle. So that was Lisa's game. She really was jealous. Well, she wasn't going to frighten me away that easily! I wasn't the wimp she'd taken me for.

'Thanks for the warning,' I said resolutely. 'But I'm sure I'll be all right.' I wished I'd got the guts to tell him how scared I really felt – underneath.

9

My Mum and the Fight

Going to school on Monday morning was awful. My stomach was churning and I felt clammy all over. I was convinced Donna and Lisa would beat me up at the first opportunity. Nothing had happened by lunchtime except that my nerve had completely broken. I remembered how determined to do battle I'd been in the park with Chas and couldn't imagine ever feeling that way again. I'd stopped worrying about how I felt about Chas; I was too busy worrying about whether I'd still be in one piece at the end of the day. I didn't even feel safe with my friends. Could they be trusted to take my side? The only really reliable person was Chas – and I didn't tend to hang around with him at school. But things were desperate. I was so jittery, I couldn't even eat my lunch.

I tracked him down in the library. He was reading an *Asterix* book.

'Hullo!' he said, looking up in surprise.

'Shhh!' said the librarian.

'Can I talk to you?' I mouthed.

Chas raised his eyebrows and put the book back on the shelf. He followed me out of the library.

'What is it?' he asked curiously.

I thought for a moment and then decided it would be better to just tell him.

'I'm scared of Lisa and Donna,' I said simply.

'Join the club,' said Chas. 'But I thought you said...'

'I was lying,' I said. Briefly, I explained about the park. 'You see,' I said when I'd finished, 'it was nothing really. But I know what they've done to other girls.'

Chas nodded. 'You need a minder,' he said.

'I've got one,' I replied. 'My mum.'

'No, in school, stupid,' he rejoined. 'Me.'

I considered the idea for a moment. No. It wouldn't work. 'Lisa would just be even more jealous,' I said.

'Yeah, but she couldn't do anything about it because I'd always be around,' he retorted with a grin.

'When I go to the loo?' I asked irritably. 'That's where people like that really get you.'

'If you're not out in three minutes, I'll phone the rescue services, OK?

'You're not taking this seriously,' I complained.

'Oh yes I am,' he said. 'I just can't think what else might work. It'd help me out too. Lisa might finally get

113

the idea that I'm not interested in her.'

'But…' I wasn't quite sure how to say what I wanted to say. 'But everyone would talk,' I said. 'You know… about us.'

'So what?' said Chas casually. 'They're talking about us anyway. Haven't you noticed? Let them get on with it. They haven't got anything better to do.'

'But…' I was astounded. I'd sort of assumed that a sensitive boy like Chas wouldn't want to be the talk of the Lower School.

'Actually,' he added, 'to be honest, all this gossip has been doing me a favour.'

'What d'you mean?' I asked suspiciously.

'Well, it's done wonders for my street cred, having all these rumours flying round about me and you. None of the boys will believe that you're not my girlfriend, so they've decided I'm not such a jerk as they thought I was.'

'I don't believe you,' I said.

'It's true,' he insisted. 'Some of them are quite jealous. I'm serious.'

I still didn't believe him but at least my appetite had come back and I just had time to bolt down my sandwiches before registration.

We had Maths first that afternoon. Chas is in a different set from me but he insisted on delivering me to the door of my classroom. I sit next to a girl called Vicky for Maths. We get on all right but I don't see her out of lessons.

'Saw you talking to Chas at lunchtime today,' she said,

as I sat down. 'Are you going out with him?'

I shook my head.

'You're just good friends?'

I nodded.

'That's nice,' she said. I could tell she didn't believe me. It was weird. Why would no one accept that Chas and I could just be friends? It made me feel like deliberately trying to prove them all wrong. I mean, even BBM is the same!

Our Maths teacher always keeps us a couple of minutes past the bell. Vicky nudged me as we were packing away.

'Hurry up,' she said. 'He's waiting for you.' She gave me a knowing smile.

Sure enough, I could see Chas through the glass panel in the door. Twenty-eight pairs of eyes seemed to watch me as I slung my bag over my shoulder and went out to meet him.

I'll never know if Lisa and Donna changed their plan. Maybe they were going to flush my head down the loo on that first Monday and were put off by Chas. Anyway, nothing happened for a couple of days. I began to wonder if I ought to tell Chas he could go off-duty. But then things began to disappear. The odd bit of homework. An exercise book. And other things began to turn up. Nasty little notes. My exercise book came back with things written on it about Chas and me. It was horrible. I mean, apart from the fact that it was a real nuisance and I was having to watch over my property like a hawk, it was really unsettling never knowing when the next little dig would be made. I hadn't a clue how to stop them but I didn't fancy letting this go on until I left school.

'Ignore it,' said Chas. 'They'll get bored soon.'

But it was pretty hard to ignore.

I wondered about telling a teacher but decided that would do no good. I mean, what could I say? 'These two girls keep writing rude things about me.' It sounded a bit pathetic. And I'm not so brilliant at looking after my property that I could always tell that it had been taken deliberately. One day I thought they'd taken my history project but then found that I'd left it at home. Anyway, wouldn't they just be even more mad with me, if I told on them? No, it would have to be me who sorted them out – somehow.

I'll tell you what I didn't do. I didn't try praying. Somehow I was so bogged down in it all and so fed up that I didn't even give praying a thought. I don't know how Chas put up with me, I was such a misery.

And then, after it had been going on for over two weeks, something happened which changed everything.

It was break time. Chas had to see a teacher about some work and I was desperate to go to the loo. I decided I'd chance it. After all, since Chas had been 'minding' me, I'd never even seen Donna and Lisa in the loos, let alone been duffed up by them.

I knew something was up as I walked through the

double doors. There was a large bunch of girls hanging around by the wall-length mirror, giggling. That wasn't unusual. But the way they started nudging each other and glancing over their shoulders at me certainly was. I carefully ignored the looks I was getting and attempted to stroll over to the loo in a calm and dignified manner. By the time I got there my cheeks were flaming. I could guess what it was all about.

Our school is very down on graffiti. I've had to cover the books Donna and Lisa have vandalized before any teacher has had a chance to notice. If anyone does write on the walls, the culprit never remains unknown for long and the penalties are severe. But there are ways of getting round rules and one cunning ruse is to write on the mirrors in felt-pen or lipstick, let everyone have a good laugh over it, and then clean it off quickly before a teacher sees. It's risky. I mean, there's always supposed to be a teacher on duty, checking that nothing awful is happening in the loos. But some teachers are more conscientious than others. If you want to scribble on the mirrors, you just have to choose the right day.

My intention was to walk out into the corridor again without so much as a glance at the mirror, even though really I wanted to brush my hair. Easier said than done.

'Hey, Kate,' someone called. 'This true then, is it?' And, sniggering, she read the mirror's message in a loud, clear voice.

It wasn't about me. I would have coped better if it was. It was something very rude about Chas.

I strode over to the mirrors. 'No, it is not,' I said tightly, and began rubbing at it furiously with my sleeve. I could see the angry colour in my face and the reflection of my tear-bright eyes. I was very aware of the circle of nudging, giggling onlookers but I had gone into overdrive. An uncontrollable fury powered my arm. So it was very unfortunate that Lisa and Donna chose that particular moment to return to remove their handiwork. I saw their reflections and turned.

'You *****!' I snarled. There was an excited gasp. I knew what they were thinking. Vicar's kid uses swear word! Wow! But I didn't care. Lisa and Donna blenched. Donna was the first to recover.

'Oooh, we are defensive, aren't we?' she cooed. 'Does that mean it's true, then?'

'You know it isn't true,' I said in a low, hard voice.

'Really?' said Donna. 'Well, don't get your knickers in a twist. I was just about to wipe it off.'

Her casual scorn wound me up even more. 'You're only doing this because Lisa's jealous,' I snapped. 'Well, Chas can't stand her so you might as well leave me and him alone.'

Slap! The sharp sound echoed around the tiled walls. I gasped, winded. I was so furious that it took me a moment to grasp that it was my face that was beginning to sting and throb but the moment I did, I reacted. Without thinking, I lunged forward and grabbed Lisa by her tie. I wanted to throttle her. She clawed at my face but I had her hair with my other hand. I was oblivious to the stunned faces surrounding us. Someone, of course, was haring off to find a teacher, but I wasn't bothered. I swung Lisa round. I'm taller than her and I managed to bear down on her so that I was crushing her against one of the wash-basins. I know I was shouting things at her, but I don't know what. She gave up on my face and tried to push me away but I was relentless, immovable, hell-bent on revenge.

I don't know what would have happened next. I certainly didn't have any clear idea of what I was trying to do to Lisa, and my wrist was beginning to hurt. But at that moment there was an appalling crumbling, creaking noise, followed by a deafening smash and Lisa slid away from me. I leapt back in horror. For one awful moment, I thought that I had broken her spine.

Instead, I had broken the wash-basin. It had been there a long time and wasn't intended to take the weight of two struggling girls. The damp, antiquated plaster had given way and the whole basin had crashed to the floor. Lisa was sitting in what remained of it. Wordlessly, I offered her a hand up. She didn't take it and Donna pushed me aside. It occurred to me to wonder what she'd been doing while I attempted to cripple her friend. People were clutching at each other in hysterical laughter, but I couldn't see the funny side. My fury had evaporated and I was left with a cold, sickly feeling of panic in the pit of my stomach.

And that was the moment that Mrs Stubbs, the Head of Lower School, arrived.

You can guess what happened. BBM was sent for. I was given a pile of boring worksheets and had to sit outside the Lower School office for the afternoon, with strict instructions not to speak to anyone. I wouldn't have dared. I mean, I'm not a real goodie-goodie but I'm usually fairly law-abiding. Lisa had been dispatched to hospital with a chunk of basin embedded in her hand. I'm afraid I wasn't sorry.

I didn't make much of the worksheets. I just kept going over and over the whole, hideous scene, trying to work out what I should have done. And what on earth I was going to say to BBM. I mean, it was bound to come out – that it had been about Chas. And then she was bound to say that I should stop seeing him. And I couldn't bear that. He's the only really close friend I've ever had. Why hadn't I ignored that mouthy girl in the loos? Why hadn't I just walked out when Donna and Lisa walked in? Why, oh why hadn't I kept my temper?

I wondered what Chas was thinking. He was sure to have heard something about what had happened. Of course, I wasn't allowed to see him. Mrs Stubbs checked up on me occasionally and told me my mother would be coming to see her after school. Presumably she told me that just to increase the agony.

At last the bell rang for the end of afternoon school. The usual gang of people on report assembled in the corridor beside me. They stared at me curiously.

'Hear you've put some girl in the hospital,' said a tall boy with ginger hair, conversationally. 'What's the vicar going to say to that, then?'

I buried my head in the work I had been set.

'Be like that then,' said the boy. 'Snooty cow.'

'She'll know pretty soon, anyway,' said another boy further down the queue and jerked his head towards the double doors at the end of the corridor.

Sure enough, BBM was just pushing her way through. I buried my head in the worksheets. It was so unfair that everyone knew who she was and what she did. Of course, every so often she's in school to do assemblies and sometimes she's brought in for social education lessons. She even gets dragged in occasionally to do counselling with particularly awkward kids. What must she be thinking now that the awkward kid was one of her own?

I think those minutes while we waited for the Head of Lower School to deal with the rest of the troublemakers were the longest of my entire life. I couldn't talk to Mum with all those other kids around, even if I had wanted to. And Mum looked ready to burst.

At last everyone had gone and we were invited into the office.

'I must say,' said Mrs Stubbs, obviously not wanting to

waste any time, 'I am extremely surprised by what has happened. I don't think Kate has ever been in serious trouble before and I'm sure this is an isolated incident, but the fact remains that a lot of damage has been done. We must make sure that there is no repetition of this sort of thing.'

She paused, but neither Mum nor I said anything.

'Well,' continued Mrs Stubbs, 'I have heard what Lisa did and she was obviously very wrong, but that does not excuse your behaviour, Kate. Have you anything you'd like to say?'

'I lost my temper,' I whispered, half choking on the tears I was trying to hold back.

'It's some silly business with a boy,' exploded Mum, scarlet-cheeked and obviously at the end of her patience.

Mrs Stubbs gave her a very hard look. 'Just a moment, please, Reverend Lofthouse,' she said. She turned to me again.

'Would you say, Kate,' she said, quite gently, 'that Lisa and Donna have been bullying you?'

I shook my head. 'Not really,' I croaked.

'Not really?' Mrs Stubbs let my words hang in the air.

Mum sighed and fidgeted impatiently.

'It would be better if you told us what they'd done,' said Mrs Stubbs.

I didn't know what to do. Should I tell? Or shouldn't I? If I told, would Donna and Lisa stop picking on people? Or would they just have it in for me? Perhaps, having shown Lisa that I could put her in the hospital, she'd leave me alone anyway?

The seconds ticked by. Mrs Stubbs seemed content to wait. Mum, however, was not.

'Excuse me, Mrs Stubbs,' she said, in a voice tight with impatience, 'I appreciate your kindness but I do not believe that Kate has been the victim of any bullying. From what you said on the phone, this all boils down to some unpleasantness about Charles Peterson. I have been foolish in allowing Kate to become so involved with him. Clearly, this is something we need to talk about at home. Once Kate has made amends for the damage she has caused and she is not seeing so much of Charles, I'm sure there will be nothing more to worry about.'

My stomach heaved. I felt as if the floor had tilted. Was this BBM? That sympathetic, tolerant, jolly mother I had once had? The one who always insisted on listening to everyone's point of view? What had happened to her?

'Kate?' said Mrs Stubbs doggedly. 'Was there anything you wanted to say?'

Well, there was, but it would have taken about a week.

'No,' I said weakly, 'except that I'm sorry about the basin.' And then, because a little flame of angry loyalty forced me to – 'And that Chas Peterson is my friend.'

After that they stitched it up fairly quickly between them. I was going to come in on a Saturday and do enough mindlessly boring, useful jobs around the school to teach me to leave the wash-basins alone in future. Mum was perfectly happy to supervise me. Well, she was bound to be, wasn't she? I mean, it'd keep me out of Chas's way for a whole day, wouldn't it?

I felt as if I would never trust her again.

I buried my head in the work I had been set.

10

My Mum and
the Rain

The one thing I wanted to do when I got home after that dreadful interview with Mrs Stubbs was to ring Chas. It was, of course, the one thing I didn't even dare to attempt.

Everything was extremely odd. Dad was home early – I suppose Mum must have rung him – and Ben and I were sent off to eat our tea in front of the television while they talked.

Ben gave me a worried look. 'You must have done something really awful, Kate,' he said.

I nodded. I was tired and weepy and guilt had kicked in. I sat in front of the television like a zombie. Then the telephone rang. I ran towards it but Mum got there first.

'I'm sorry, Charles,' Mum was saying frostily. 'She's not available to speak to you at the moment.'

'That's a lie!' I yelled, as Mum put down the phone.

Then I flung myself on the sofa and howled. Ben, bless him, knelt on the floor beside me and helplessly patted my shoulder.

I was sent to my room after tea. 'We'll talk to you later,' said Mum. It was lucky for Ben that it was his Cubs night. I sat and struggled to write about everything that had happened, while half-hearing the argument that was raging downstairs.

I got a fairly clear idea of what was being said. Mum was insisting that I shouldn't be so involved with that boy and Dad was equally insistent that she was over-reacting. At last they must have reached some sort of agreement, because Dad called me down.

They were in the kitchen. Mum was leaning against the sink, her face all hot-looking and red and blotchy.

'Right, Kate…' she started as I walked in and sat down at the table.

Dad interrupted her. 'I thought…?' he said with a quelling glance.

'Oh yes,' she said. 'Sorry.'

Dad sat down opposite me.

'OK Kate,' he said gently. 'How about telling us what happened?'

And so I told them. I was too tired to work out what I should and shouldn't say any more. And anyway, Dad makes it easy to talk. He doesn't interrupt; he just nods and grunts and makes little encouraging noises in all the right places. Mum says he does more good listening to people while he's doing their hair than she does with all her visiting. So I told him everything, right from that meeting in the park with Donna and Lisa. When I got to the bit where Lisa slapped me across the face and I grabbed her by the tie, I went very red.

'I know what you're going to say,' I said defensively. 'Do not repay evil for evil or insult with insult – but what was I supposed to do? Let her rearrange my face?'

They looked at me.

'OK,' I sighed. 'I could have tried praying. But I can't see what good it would have done. I mean, what could God really have done? Not even Chas knew where I was.'

'Who knows?' mused Dad. 'You'll never find out what God can do, if you never give him a chance.'

And then I remembered my cry for help in the park. It had only been ever such a little prayer – if you could even call it a prayer. But it had been Donna and Lisa who went sprawling in the mud, not me. Maybe I was going to have to give this prayer business a bit more attention.

'So you see,' I said, when I'd finally finished my story, 'you can't really blame Chas for any of it. In fact, if it weren't for Chas, things might have been a lot worse with Donna and Lisa.'

'If it weren't for Chas, Lisa and Donna would never have paid you any attention,' said Mum firmly. 'You're far too young to cope with all this sort of thing. Just look what a mess you're in already. Lisa has had to go to hospital and a wash-basin is hanging off the wall.'

'But it's not fair,' I wailed. 'Why can't Chas be my friend, just because he's a boy? Why does everyone think he's got to be my boyfriend?'

'It's the way of the world, love,' said Dad, with a shrug. 'We just don't want you to get hurt, that's all.'

'But so long as Lisa and Donna leave me alone, I'm not going to get hurt,' I retorted. 'If you won't let me see Chas, Lisa will have won!'

'I think we're forgetting,' said Mum, her colour rising again, 'that all this has led to very serious trouble at school, trouble which would never have occurred if Kate hadn't been so involved with Charles…'

My temper began to slip. 'I am not involved with Charles,' I interrupted rudely. 'I'm friends with Chas!'

'… if Kate hadn't been so involved with Charles,' she continued, as if I hadn't spoken. 'I might also add that, despite our patience, Kate is choosing to be thoroughly uncooperative and rude.'

'Now, Jo…' began Dad but it was too late. I had had enough.

'I am not uncooperative and rude,' I shouted. 'I just want to keep the one real friend I've got! You've no idea what it's like trying to make friends when your mum's always popping up in assembly to talk about God!' (This was not strictly true, but it sounded convincing.) 'And now you're trying to take him away! Well, I won't let you. I'll carry on seeing him whether you like it or not! You can't stop me when we're at school!'

And with that, I stormed out of the kitchen and up to my bedroom.

'You see?' I heard Mum say to Dad as I stamped up the stairs.

Things were distinctly frosty the next day. Neither Mum nor Dad had come to talk to me after I walked out on them, although they both stuck their heads round my door to say goodnight. They were probably plotting their next move. Breakfast was very uncomfortable, with Mum slamming around and Ben keeping his head well down. I don't think I've ever left for school so early. Apart from anything else, I was desperate to see Chas. I had to pour it all out to someone and I knew he would listen.

He was waiting by the school gate. I could have hugged him.

'They've let you out then?' he said, with a grin.

I pulled a face. 'Only just. And I'm not supposed to talk to the enemy.'

'Who? Lisa and Donna? Well, you wouldn't want to, would you?'

'No, idiot,' I said, exasperated, completely forgetting that BBM's suspicions were unknown to him. 'It's you that I'm not supposed to have anything to do with.'

'Me?' said Chas, in amazement. 'What did I do wrong?'

'Oh,' I said, clapping my hand over my mouth. 'Of course. You don't know.'

'Don't know what?' said Chas, looking as if he'd like to give me a good shake.

'Well,' I said slowly, 'you're never going to believe this…'

'Believe what?' said Chas. 'Come on, quick. The suspense is killing me.'

'Well, shut up and listen, then,' I said impatiently. 'The thing is…' I paused dramatically before dropping my bombshell. 'My mum's just as bad as all the kids at school. She thinks that we're secretly going out together.'

Chas snorted. 'Is that all?' he said, in disgust. 'All that build up for that? I've known that for ages.'

I was put out. Why was he always one jump ahead of me? 'Well, I thought it was quite important,' I said in a small voice.

'Doesn't bother me,' said Chas, with a shrug. 'I've told you before. If that's what people want to think, let them. We can still be friends, can't we?'

'But that's just it,' I said crossly. 'We can't. That's why she wouldn't let you speak to me on the phone last night. She says if I wasn't so involved with you, Lisa would never have taken any notice of me and the wash-basin would still be on the wall! She says I've to stop seeing so much of you.'

'O-o-h,' said Chas slowly, the light dawning. 'I see.'

I studied his face, trying to work out what he was thinking.

'Well?' I said impatiently. 'I don't think that's fair. And I'm not going to put up with it. Are you?'

For one awful moment, I thought he might just walk quietly away.

But he didn't. 'No,' he said, with a slight toss of his fringe. 'Neither am I. I don't see why I should.'

By the time the bell went, we had made our plan.

All day long, people kept coming up to me.

'She's a real pig, that Lisa,' said one girl sympathetically.

'Serves her right, what you did to her,' said another. 'She's always picking on people.'

There were a lot of jokes as well.

'Wouldn't like to meet you on a dark night,' said a great hulk of a boy in Year 11. He throws the hammer for the county. I felt like quite a heroine, but I didn't think Mum or Dad would be impressed. Brute force is never their way of solving a problem and secretly I was ashamed that it had been mine. I wondered what would have happened if I'd prayed instead of trying to throttle Lisa. But now I would never know.

Lisa herself wasn't in school and I only saw Donna once. She ostentatiously ignored me but I noticed that she didn't seem to have another friend to hang around with. I wondered if I'd have any more trouble from them. I had a feeling that might be the end of it.

'I hate that cow Lisa,' said Vicky at the beginning of

Maths. 'She's always sneered at me because we're not that well off. She used to give me hell when we were at primary school.'

I nodded sympathetically.

'What are they making you do about that sink, then?' she continued. 'Have your mum and dad got to pay for it?'

I shook my head. 'I've just got to come in and do loads of boring jobs tomorrow,' I told her as casually as I could manage. 'And promise I'll never be so naughty again, of course.'

Vicky laughed. 'I'll come and help you if you like,' she said, equally casually. 'I've got nothing much to do this weekend.'

'Oh, you can't do that,' I said hurriedly. 'I mean, it's really kind of you to offer, but…'

'Then I'll come,' said Vicky decidedly. 'You deserve it. It was time someone stood up to those two. Here, want a piece of gum?'

I took the gum guiltily. It didn't seem right to be basking in all this praise. I wasn't proud of what I had done, after all. Deep down I had wanted to find a better way.

But I kept quiet about that. Instead, I told Vicky the Plan.

The next day, even though it was Saturday, BBM woke me at the usual time. She brought me a cup of tea in bed. I suppose it was a sort of peace offering. 'Up you get then,' she said, not unkindly. 'You might as well get started. It's going to be a long day.'

I gave her a sour look. I wasn't feeling very forgiving.

'Are you just going to sit and watch me?' I asked coldly.

'Of course not,' she said, surprised. 'I'm going to help. You're my daughter. I suppose I bear some sort of responsibility for all this.'

'So it isn't all Chas's fault,' I muttered under my breath.

'Sorry?' said Mum.

'Oh, nothing,' I said.

I thought about the Plan. Ben was in on it too. I went to wake him up.

After breakfast, BBM cycled off to get the key from the caretaker. They don't let just anyone have the key, but BBM almost counts as a member of staff. Our school used to be two, but they were joined together to make one about twenty years ago and the caretaker's bungalow is on the Upper School site. My menial jobs were all going to be in the Lower School so I was to walk down and wait for Mum there. Ben came with me.

'What's all this?' said BBM, as she got off her bike some time later. By then there were four of us waiting for her by the school gate. Me, Ben, Vicky – and Chas.

'We came to help Kate,' said Vicky brightly.

'Because she's our friend,' added Chas.

'That's OK, isn't it, Mum?' said Ben sweetly. 'That's loving your neighbour, isn't it? Like it says in the Bible?'

BBM's lips twitched. I breathed a sigh of relief. She wasn't going to bawl us out. But then how could she?

I mean, what could she say to that?

'Well,' she said briskly, refusing to rise to the bait. 'I'm sure Kate will appreciate your help. The caretaker has given me a long list of jobs that need doing, so if anyone wants to change his or her mind, they'd better say so now.'

No one did, of course. We were all there to prove a point. Even Vicky. I'd had a long talk with her the day before. She's nice. And she understood.

We worked harder than I've ever worked in my life before. There were old desks to sand down and varnish, there was several years' worth of litter to clear out from beneath some slatted stairs, there was an old store cupboard full of junk that had to be completely emptied – the list went on and on. By the time we stopped for lunch, we were all absolutely filthy and I, at least, was exhausted. I expect everyone else was too. We hadn't wasted any time. We wanted to prove to BBM that Chas and I were sensible people whom she could trust. She seemed to think that all we wanted to do was drip around together holding hands and kissing. If we showed her that we were just as happy with Ben along too, she might get rid of that stupid idea. It was a lucky bonus that Vicky came too.

We didn't say much while we were eating our sandwiches. I think we were all too tired.

'Is there much more to do?' I asked, at last.

BBM shook her head. 'There's just the hall floor to polish and then that's it.'

134

I breathed a sigh of relief. I was aching all over.

'Was Kate supposed to do all that on her own?' enquired Chas. 'It seems rather a lot.'

BBM shook her head. 'Oh no,' she said, with a wicked chuckle. 'The caretaker just said that Kate must do as much as she could. I expect she'd only have managed half of it in the whole day on her own, with just me. But since she'd got such a willing band of friends…'

Her voice tailed off, silenced by the venomous looks she was getting. 'Well, I did help,' she said apologetically.

'Can we forget about the floor-polishing then?' asked Ben slyly.

'No,' I said firmly. 'Well, I'm going to do it anyway.'

'And so am I,' said Chas and Vicky together.

'Oh, OK,' sighed Ben. 'Let's get on with it then. Only I want Chas to play Lemmings with me later.'

At last we had finished. We packed up our things and limped out into the pouring rain.

'Yuk,' said BBM. 'I hate cycling in the rain. I always end up with wet knickers.'

Chas and Vicky choked. Even I laughed. It was a relief to have her back to normal. I decided I could cope better with being continually embarrassed than being frozen out.

BBM gave us all a withering look. 'From the puddles, you idiots,' she said. 'Mountain bikes don't have proper mud-guards.'

'You could have some put on,' said Chas.

'Could I?' said BBM, as she swung her leg over the cross-bar. 'I never thought of that.'

I caught Chas's eye and burst out laughing but BBM was halfway down the road by then.

'She ought to wear a helmet,' said Chas critically.

'She says it spoils her hair,' said Ben.

Huh! I thought to myself. So much for inner beauty!

We all went back to our house. I didn't think Mum could object to that, not after Chas had worked so hard, and not with Vicky there too. Mum wasn't back when we arrived, so Chas and Ben started rooting through the cupboards for food while Vicky and I got cleaned up. It was a good half-hour later and we were gorging ourselves on chocolate digestives and crisps and lemonade when I suddenly began to wonder where Mum had got to…

'She'll be fine,' said Ben, reaching for his fifth biscuit. 'She'll be having a nice cup of tea with the caretaker or something.'

We decided to play Mousetrap. It's a really silly game, not worth setting up for just two people, so we hadn't played it for ages. We were soon falling about laughing. I suppose we were all over-tired. The most stupid things seemed hilarious.

Then the phone rang. 'Bother!' I said, wincing as I struggled to my feet. I had stiffened up after all that work. 'It'll probably be Mum telling us to switch the oven on.'

By the time I returned to the sitting-room, all the

laughter had drained out of me.

'What's the matter, Kate?' said Chas, seeing my face. His hand froze, mid-throw. I clung to the door-frame. My whole body was trembling.

'Th-that was Dad,' I said shakily. 'He's at the hospital.'

I looked from one shocked face to another. The colour had gone from Ben's. Even his lips had turned a funny greyish-pink. I could hardly get any more words out.

'Is it…?' Ben couldn't complete his question.

'It's Mum,' I said, with an effort. 'She's had an accident.'

11

My Mum and Me

'Dad says we're to stay here,' I said, when I'd sat down, had a good howl and been mopped up by Vicky and Chas. 'But I can't. I'll go mad waiting to hear if she's all right.'

'Didn't your dad know?' asked Chas, surprised.

'Not really,' I said, beginning to sniff again. 'He was just phoning to let us know where he was – and why Mum isn't back yet. He said something about skidding in the wet and multiple injuries and that was all. It sounds dreadful – multiple injuries.'

'Oh, that often sounds worse than it is,' said Vicky knowledgeably. 'It could be just a broken rib and a few bruises, once they've cleaned her up. My uncle's a paramedic,' she added, by way of explanation.

'But it could mean she's broken every bone in her body,' I said, my voice beginning to rise hysterically. 'It could mean she's going to…'

'Oh shut up!' said Ben fiercely. I'd somewhat forgotten

about Ben. He was biting his lip hard and looked very close to tears. 'You'll have to do something, Kate,' he said, a bit desperately. 'I can't just sit here and wait either.'

But I didn't know what to do. My brain felt like soup. I suppose it was the shock.

'I'll ring my mum,' said Chas, with decision. 'Perhaps she could run us all up to the hospital. We'll probably have to just sit around and wait there too, but anything's better than doing nothing.'

I breathed a huge sigh of relief. Just then, Mrs Charming Peterson seemed exactly who we needed. Competent, efficient, forthright... the sort of person you could imagine marching into the hospital and saying, 'Now look here. We need some answers and we need them now!' And because she always looks so elegant and well-bred, you can bet your bottom dollar she'd get some action. Well, that's what I thought.

Twenty minutes later, sitting in the Petersons' immaculate car, I tried to collect my thoughts. 'Pray,' I told myself. 'That's what Mum would say. Just pray – and pray properly – not just "Dear God, help!"'

But I couldn't. My thoughts splurged in all sorts of unexpected directions. I found myself rather enviously admiring the dust-free dashboard and the pristine upholstery. No spilt apple-juice stains here. No used tissues stuffed down the sides of the seats. I shuddered, remembering Gran's ride home from Oxford. Thank goodness she hadn't done any damage! And the next moment I was thinking about Gran. What were we going to tell her? The shock might kill her. But tomorrow was Sunday. Wouldn't she be expecting to come to lunch? And who would do the service for Mum?

With a jolt, I realized that we had arrived at the hospital. I was cross with myself. What had I been thinking of? What did it matter if the Petersons' car was cleaner than ours, when Mum might be…? I couldn't complete the sentence, even in my head.

I followed Mrs Peterson's navy blue, business-like figure across the car park and through the doors of Accident and Emergency, as if in a dream. We sat down in the reception area while Chas's mum went to join the queue at the desk. Vicky began to rummage through the pile of old magazines. Chas, Ben and I just sat.

More waiting, I thought glumly. I felt like running back out into the car park and screaming. But Ben was sitting close up against me with his thumb in his mouth. It made me ache for him. He hadn't sucked his thumb for a couple of years. Gently, I put my arm round him.

'You all right?' asked Chas gruffly.

I shook my head. 'I want to scream,' I said irritably. 'My brain isn't working properly. I tried to pray in the car but I couldn't concentrate.' I stopped short. I'd never talked to Chas about God or praying or anything like that. I suppose I was a bit worried it might put him off me. He knew what my mum did – didn't everyone? – and I had left it at that.

'Oh, I was praying,' said Chas easily. 'Want me to do it again?'

'I didn't know you prayed,' I said, in astonishment.

''Course I do,' he said casually. 'Why not? Anyway, how did you think I survived living with my mum?'

I half-smiled and then realized it probably wasn't a joke. But this was no time to go into the whys and wherefores.

'Go on, then,' I whispered. 'Maybe it'll help me concentrate if you're doing it too.' I shut my eyes tight and hugged Ben a bit closer.

'Dear Lord,' started Chas clearly.

My eyes opened with a jerk. 'I didn't think you meant out loud!' I hissed, looking round hurriedly to see if anyone had noticed.

Chas gave me his 'Are you seriously deranged?' look. I was beginning to get used to it.

'Why on earth not?' he said. 'I thought you'd want to hear what I said. And it might keep your mind off things. You know what, Kate? Your mum's right about you. You're always too worried about what other people think. Now shut up, will you? And concentrate.'

'You're getting as bad as Mum,' I grumbled, but I let him get on with it. After all, I could always pretend I wasn't with him – well, unless Vicky noticed, but she was deep in a girls' magazine.

'Dear Lord,' he prayed. 'We're really worried about Kate and Ben's mum. Please let her be all right. If she's hurt herself badly, let her get better quickly. And please help Kate and Ben and me to feel better. Oh – and Mr Lofthouse too. Amen.'

'Do you feel bad, then?' I asked stupidly.

I got the look again. 'Well, I don't exactly feel brilliant,' he said. 'I do actually like your mum, you know.'

'Oh,' I said. 'Well, thanks.'

We sat there awkwardly for a few minutes. My mind was racing. Maybe this praying thing wasn't such a big deal after all. Maybe loads of people were at it all the time, without me realizing. Mum always said you could do it any place, any time, but somehow I always thought that wasn't real praying. Real praying was when you sat down quietly for a good, long time and got serious about it. Well, Chas didn't seem to think so. So maybe that quick 'Help! Help!' in the park really was the reason that Lisa and Donna hadn't duffed me up there and then.

'I need to go to the loo,' said Ben, a bit plaintively.

'I'll come with you,' said Chas.

I watched them go. Then I had an idea. 'Vicky,' I said. 'I'm just going to the loo as well, OK?'

She nodded absently and I left.

It was exactly the sort of place I needed. It had a nice solid door with no gaps at the top and bottom. No one would hear me in there. Except God.

I put the lid down and sat on it. I cleared my throat. 'Dear God,' I said quietly. 'Now, you know I'm not too sure about this praying business. Well, to be honest, I'm not too sure about you actually. But if it was you who helped me out in the park, then thanks very much.' I stopped. I was feeling better. My thoughts had stopped zig-zagging around in ten different directions at once. I felt surprisingly calm. Perhaps Chas's prayer for us to feel better had been answered already. And if that one had been answered, maybe…?

Better get on and pray some more, I told myself. Although it wasn't fair to hog the loo for too long.

When I got back to reception, Mrs Peterson was at the front of the queue.

'What happened to you?' said Chas. 'I was just about to come and see if you were all right. Vicky's gone off to phone her mum.'

'Sorry,' I said, sitting down quickly. 'I'm fine now. I didn't realize I'd been gone so long.'

And I hadn't realized. I must have been praying for about ten minutes, I suppose, mostly in my head but sometimes out loud. Once I'd started, it was difficult to stop. There seemed to be an awful lot I wanted to say and I was enjoying it in a strange sort of way. It was a bit like pouring out my troubles over my keyboard, except that I really had a feeling of someone who understood me listening to my thoughts.

The next moment, I heard Mrs Peterson thanking the receptionist and then she was coming towards us. I stood up, dragging Ben with me and gripping his hand hard. My brain was steely calm; my tummy felt as if ten thousand tadpoles were running riot inside.

'Is she…?' I still couldn't finish my sentences.

'She's alive, Kate,' said Mrs Peterson, smiling kindly, 'but I'm afraid they won't tell me any more than that. Apparently, your father is going up with her to her ward and then they've asked that he comes straight down to see you. So we have to wait here. I'm sorry. I wish I could have got a bit more out of them than that, but they're very strict about giving out information.'

'But she's our mum,' I protested, bursting into a storm of tears. 'They ought to tell us. She doesn't belong to them!'

Mrs Peterson put her arm round me and cooed. That's the only word I can think of for it. Yuk! I felt like babies must feel when doting old ladies chuck them under their chins! And despite the fact that I was wailing like a three-year-old, her perfume nearly knocked me out. That probably did more to make me pull myself together than anything else! I shook her off ungratefully.

'Sorry,' I said, with a sniff and a hiccup. 'Sorry to be such an idiot.'

'No one thinks you're an idiot, dear,' murmured Mrs Charming. 'It's only to be expected.'

Chas passed me a crumpled tissue and I blew my nose noisily. Poor Chas. I guess I'd pray a lot more if I had to put up with that. But maybe I'll be praying more from now on anyway.

So we sat down to wait again. I'm sure it's a deliberate hospital policy, all this making you wait. By the time you get to see anyone or hear anything, you're so exhausted and bored brainless that you'd lick the doctor's boots in gratitude – even if he told you they'd lost your nearest and dearest somewhere between X-ray and the plaster room. We played I-Spy. We played Scissors-Paper-Stone. We played every single game we'd ever played on a long car journey and invented some of our own – and still Dad didn't come down to see us.

'I'm really sorry, Kate,' said Vicky. 'I'm going to have to go home or my mum'll go mad. Promise you'll ring me as soon as you know...' She stopped. It was difficult to find something to say.

'It's OK, Vicky,' I said and got up to walk with her to the big swing-doors. 'Thanks for everything. I really appreciate it.'

She nodded. 'See you soon,' she said and hurried off into the rain. I walked slowly back to the waiting area.

Mrs Peterson went back to the desk. We watched her face slowly turning an unnatural shade of puce as the receptionist made a few hurried phone calls.

'What is it?' I demanded, hurrying over to join her.

'The receptionist thinks the message that we are here may not have got through,' said Chas's mum, tight-lipped with irritation. 'In which case, your father will probably have gone home.'

'I'm terribly sorry...' the receptionist began to say, when she was interrupted by a great yell from Ben.

'Dad!' he shouted and, sure enough, Dad had burst through the swing-doors at the entrance to Accident and Emergency and was scanning the waiting area worriedly. His face was drawn and his hair was coming loose from its ponytail.

'There you are,' he said, in relief, hurrying over in response to Ben's yell. 'Why on earth didn't you stay at home like I told you to, Kate? It's a good job Chas had the sense to leave a note to say where you'd gone. I can do without any more worry for one day.'

Then he remembered Mrs Peterson.

'Oh, I am sorry,' he said tiredly. 'I don't mean to sound rude or ungrateful.'

Chas's mum nodded understandingly. She looked ready to coo over him too, but I interrupted before she had the chance.

'What about Mum?' I demanded. 'Is she going to be all right?'

I never knew a split second could last so long.

'Yes,' said Dad firmly. 'Yes, Kate, she is. She's going to be pretty poorly for a few days and it's going to be a long time before she's back on her feet, but by Christmas, she should be just about better.'

I took a great leap and hurled myself onto Dad's chest.

'Hey, steady on,' he gasped. 'Don't knock me flying and fracture my skull too.'

'Oh Dad,' I said into his neck. 'I'll never moan about her again. I'm so glad she's going to be all right.'

He hugged me closer. 'Really?' he said. 'I'll remind you of that when she's back on her feet.'

'Is that what Mum's done then?' asked Ben plaintively. 'Has she broken her skull?'

Dad pushed me gently aside and drew Ben close.

'Yes,' he said, putting an arm round his shoulders. 'She was going round a downhill bend too fast in all that rain, misjudged it, hit the kerb and went head first over her handle bars into a wall.'

I had to sit down. The very thought made me feel sick. 'She could easily have broken her neck. Or died from concussion.'

'Yes,' said Dad, nodding. 'She could have been killed. As it is she's got cuts and bruises and a fracture down the back of her skull. She wears a helmet after this or I'll sell her bike. Though actually nobody'd buy her bike at the moment. It didn't come off very well either.'

'When can we see her?' asked Ben impatiently.

'Not just now,' said Dad gently. 'She needs to sleep – and you wouldn't want to see her anyway. I've never seen anyone look quite so green. We'll see how she is tomorrow. What d'you say to us all going down to Pizza Hut? I don't feel up to cooking tonight.'

'I'm not sure…' started Mrs Peterson.

'Yeah!' interrupted Ben immediately. 'I'm starving. And can I have a go on the Ice Cream Factory for pudding?'

'Oh Ben,' I said, in disgust. 'All you think about is your stomach.'

But really I was glad he *wanted* to think about his stomach. We'd been in that hospital for nearly two-and-a-half hours and Ben hadn't complained he was hungry once. That just showed how bad he'd been feeling.

We were allowed in to see Mum for just a few minutes the next day, but she wasn't up to talking. She whispered our names and tried to smile, but she obviously felt absolutely terrible. We crept away and wished we hadn't bothered to come. It was awful to see her lying there, so still and helpless, when we were used to her bossing us and everyone else around. Poor Gran would have to wait a while for her next Sunday lunch at our house!

Flowers and plants and chocolates and cards poured in. We could have opened a couple of nice shops. Dad gave us a huge pile of notecards and told us to get busy with the thank yous.

'Oh Dad,' groaned Ben. 'Do we have to?'

'Well, who else is going to do it?' he said reasonably. 'Your mum's not going to be anything like normal for a good six weeks and she won't need any extra work, even then. Put on a good video and write them while you're watching. Just don't tell your mum when she's better!'

We roped in Chas, of course. And even Vicky wrote about twenty. In fact, the four of us did a pretty good job of running the house for those first few days before Mum came home. Dad seemed to spend all his time at the hospital or on the phone, so after school we cooked, we shopped, we hoovered, we tidied, we did the washing, we answered the door. We've been so busy I haven't had the energy to worry, let alone spend much time on this keyboard. Vicky's been really enjoying herself. All her brothers and sisters are much older than her, so she's pretty lonely at home – and fed up with being told what to do! I like her a lot. Looks like I might end up with two really close friends!

It was amazing how little Chas knew about anything. He'd never loaded a washing-machine or so much as ironed a pillow-case. He couldn't find anything in the supermarket, and he even had difficulty opening a tin of beans!

'Mum does everything,' he said apologetically. 'I wish she didn't, but she does.'

I pondered over it later. Dad didn't think it was fair for

us to have to do all the housework for the whole time that Mum was convalescing, so he was thinking of getting someone in to help – but we could still do some of it. How on earth would Chas and his dad manage if Mrs Peterson ever had an accident? At least Chas could open a tin of beans now and he was quite a whizz with the hoover, but there was a long way to go. For the umpteenth time since the accident, I thanked God that I'd still got my mum. Mums could certainly come a lot worse.

By the end of the week, she was home. She was still as weak as a kitten and, on the rare occasions that she got up, she moved like Frankenstein's monster, but she was home. A bed had been set up for her in the sitting-room as she couldn't manage the stairs, and as soon as she'd been settled in it, she fell asleep, exhausted just by the journey home. It's going to be a long time before she's doing her workout again, I thought sadly, remembering the scene with Chas in that very room.

But that evening Dad sent me in to see her.

'She's got something she wants to say,' he said. 'But I'm not letting her have longer than five minutes, OK?'

I nodded and tiptoed into the sitting-room. Mum looked very odd lying flat with the covers pulled up to her chin, and her spiky hair rather greasy and matted on the pillow. She'd lost weight too, of course, and her face looked strangely naked, now that it was thinner and she didn't have her earrings. Ben's kitten was curled up beside her.

I thought about Fergus's funeral and I smiled. I could see the funny side now.

I knelt down close to Mum so that she didn't have to speak above a whisper if she didn't want to.

'You should have worn a helmet,' I said, for no particular reason except that I was wishing it hadn't happened.

'Thanks Kate,' she said, in a voice I recognized. 'Thanks a lot. And if you say anything pointed about inner beauty while I'm lying here unable to defend myself, I will hold it against you for the rest of your life. So there!' And she stuck out her tongue at me.

I laughed. I couldn't help it. It was such a relief. She was just the same as she'd always been – just a bit quieter and flat on her back.

'That's right, have a good laugh,' she said resentfully. 'Go on. Kick a dog when it's down. Honestly. And I was going to apologize to you.'

But she wasn't really cross.

'Oh Mum,' I said, a lump suddenly rising in my throat. 'I do love you, you know.'

'Huh,' she chuntered. 'You've a funny way of showing it. Anyway, your dad'll throw you out in a minute so shut up and let me speak.'

There was a silence.

'Go on then,' I said helpfully.

'Give me a break, Kate,' said Mum. 'It's not easy saying sorry for being a complete idiot when you're flat on your back and your head feels like there's an ice-pick wedged in it. But I am sorry. For not trusting you. And for making things hard for you. And for the things I've said about you and Chas. You made your point very well last Saturday.' She blinked a couple of times. 'I was proud of you, Kate. And ashamed of myself. I think I panicked at the thought of you turning into a teenager. Pity I went and smashed my head in before I got chance to tell you.'

'That's all right,' I whispered, stroking the duvet where it hid her arm. 'I'm proud of you, too, really. I prayed and prayed you'd get better. 'Cos I wouldn't want you any different. Honest. I knew that the moment Dad rang and said you'd had an accident. I mean, no one else has got a mum like you. I wouldn't change a thing. Even the way you go on and on about God and inner beauty and loving your neighbour. Even your hair. Even your earrings. Even your electric pink leggings – oh sorry, I forgot. They've split.'

Mum's lips twitched. 'Even…' she said, 'even my big bum?'

I giggled and pulled the duvet straight.

'Even,' I said, 'even your mega-enormous, whopping, gigantic, unbelievable, mind-boggling bum.'

'Thanks Kate,' said BBM. 'Thanks a lot. Thanks for the vote of confidence. I'll remember that the next time my leggings split in public.'

Clumsily she slid her hand out from under the covers and reached for mine.

'I love you too, you know, Kate,' she said seriously, summoning up the strength to give my fingers a gentle squeeze.

I grinned. 'I know you do, silly,' I said, and, leaning over, I kissed her, just as the door opened and Dad called me away.

Also available from Lion Publishing

My Mum and the Gruesome Twosome

Meg Harper

'I can't believe it! At her age – she's gone and GOT PREGNANT! I haven't told anyone yet. It's too embarrassing. I might tell Vicky tomorrow but I don't expect much sympathy from her. My last hope is Chas – surely I can rely on him to understand?'

Being a teenager is difficult enough – without suddenly finding out that your mum is pregnant.

And then there's new girl, Carly. Chas seems a bit too keen to help her settle in, and Kate feels that her whole life is falling apart…

ISBN 0 7459 4829 4

My Mum and the Hound from Hell

Meg Harper

'OK. That does it. I've finally had it. I've survived
thirteen years living in this demented household
but I can't take it any more. Mum wants to add
a dog to this overcrowded collection of weirdos!
The last thing we need is a dog!'

Kate predicts trouble when her eccentric
mum adopts a friendly but badly behaved pet.
And she's right! Rover causes chaos wherever he
goes. Add to that the arrival of a gorgeous new
boy at school and the very odd behaviour of her
best friend, Chas, and Kate starts wondering if
she's going crazy…

ISBN 0 7459 4799 9

The Ghost in the Gallery

Meg Harper

'Tell me about the Great House – all the interesting stuff. Any secret passages? Any ghosts? Any skeletons hidden under the floorboards?'

Meriel turned. There was a slight gleam in her eye. 'There is a ghost, actually,' she said. 'The story's horrible. Are you sure you want to hear it?'

Resentful of the newcomers in her home, Meriel is desperate to get rid of them.

ISBN 0 7459 4589 9

Our Kid

Ann Pilling

'Bright lad wanted for *Spotlight* and other
deliveries.'

    A paper round is just what Frank is looking
for – some money will solve all his problems.
The job takes Frank to a new part of town where
he makes some unexpected friends and also
stumbles on a mystery. In a surprising and moving
climax, Frank discovers some of the extraordinary
things people will do for love.

'Sensitively written and thoroughly readable.'

The Guardian

ISBN 0 7459 4293 8

Midnight Blue

Pauline Fisk

Winner of the Smarties Book Prize

'As Bonnie rose, the sun's warmth turned the dark
skin of the fiery balloon midnight blue. She flew
straight up. Then the smooth sky puckered into
cloth-of-blue and drew aside. They passed straight
through...'

This compelling and mysterious fantasy tells
the story of Bonnie, whose fragile happiness with
her mother is under threat. With the help of new-
found friends Bonnie finds a world beyond the
sky, where everything is a strange reflection of the
world she has left. Here she faces challenges and
choices which could change her life for ever.

'Deeply satisfying... complex and haunting.'
The Sunday Times

ISBN 0 7459 4739 5

Them

Fay Sampson

'Nothing good is ever going to happen to me
again!' The snatch of a song floated through
Berlewen's mind: *One new morning our Prince
will appear...* 'What Prince?' she said aloud,
angrily. 'There's only THEM!'

Berlewen is trapped in a past she has not
chosen, denied any modern technology. Honesty,
her servant, longs to free her family, now enslaved
in a weapons factory. Only Map, the bootboy,
seems sure of the freedom promised in the
ancient song.

'Fay Sampson is a writer of great invention
and power.'

Books for Keeps

ISBN 0 7459 4670 4

All Lion books are available from your local
bookshop, or can be ordered via our website
or from Marston Book Services. For a free
catalogue, showing the complete list of titles
available, please contact:

Customer Services
Marston Book Services
PO Box 269
Abingdon
Oxon
OX14 4YN

Tel: 01235 465500
Fax: 01235 465555

Our website can be found at:
www.lion-publishing.co.uk